Dark Verses & Light

Johns Hopkins: Poetry and Fiction
John T. Irwin, General Editor

Poetry Titles in the Series

Dark Verses

&

Light

Tom Disch

The Johns Hopkins University Press

Baltimore & London

This book has been brought to publication with the generous assistance of the Albert Dowling Trust.

The Johns Hopkins University Press
701 West 40th Street, Baltimore, Maryland 21211
The Johns Hopkins Press Ltd., London

∞ The paper used in this book meets the minimum requirements
of American National Standard for Information Sciences—Permanence
of Paper for Printed Library Materials, ANSI Z39.48-1984.

Library of Congress Cataloging-in-Publication Data
Disch, Thomas M.
Dark verses and light / Tom Disch.
        p.   cm.—(Johns Hopkins, poetry and fiction)
ISBN 0-8018-4191-7 (alk. paper).—ISBN 0-8018-4192-5 (pbk.: alk. paper)
        I. Title. II. Series.
PS3554.I8D37 1991
811'.54—dc20   90-21344

Some of these poems first appeared in the following magazines and anthologies: *Amazing Stories, Boulevard, Contact II, Grand Street, Inquiry, Lake Street Review, Little Magazine, New Republic, Open Places, Paris Review,* the *PEN Bulletin, Quarto* (UK), *TLS, Transatlantic Review, Tribune* (UK), *Umbral, Witness, Light Year '85, Berkley Showcase,* and the Yorkcon program book (UK). "A Questionnaire" appeared in *Poetry.*

For John Sutherland

Contents

III

IV

1234

The Snake in the Manger: A Christmas Legend

Low in the East one winter night
A Star appeared, so big and bright
That animals for miles around
Looked on amazed and pawed the ground.

"Is it a sign?" the cows did low,
"And if it is, where must we go?"
"To Bethlehem," some seraphs bid them
Just as a burst of glory hid them.   8

"To Be-eh-eh-thlehem?" a black sheep bleated.
"To Bethlehem," the Star repeated,
"Where you will find within the manger
Something than fiction even stranger."

"And what is that?" "Just go and see,"
The Star replied peremptorily.
And so the whole menagerie
Set off at once for far Judea.   16

They traversed pastures white with snow,
Where they were joined by a fox and a crow;
Then by the marge of a marshy lake,
Spreading the news to duck and drake.

They followed the slopes of Ararat,
Where a starving dog and a mangey cat
Were added to the pilgrim throng—
And as they marched they sang a song.   24

"The cows that graze, the lambs that bleat,
And every chicken you may meet
From Palestine to lush Samoa,
All owe their lives to dear old Noah,

"Who brought us safe to Ararat
And gave us feed and made us fat.
So praise him now, and praise his Lord,
Who said to take us all on board."   32

Thus with pious moo and bark
The animals filed by the Ark,
Which moldered on the mountain's height,
All drifted over and ghostly white.

At last they got where they were going
On a cold dark night with the North Wind blowing,
And if sleet wasn't sleeting, then snow was snowing.
And lo! in the night a lamp was glowing,   40

And three Wise Men were kneeling down
Before a Fair Lady in a blue gown,
And in the Lady's arms a Child
Cooed and burbled and wriggled and smiled.

"The darling! the treasure!" declared a cow.
"I wish I had a camera now!"
"Just look at Him," an old hen clucked.
"If He's not God, then I'll be plucked."   48

A rooster crowed, as for the Sun:
"Now listen to me, everyone!
I know now why we're in Judea.
These Wise Men have the right idea.

"*We* cannot give what's bought and sold—
No myrrh or frankincense or gold—
But we can give from what we've got:
Even our little may help a lot."   56

4

The cows looked grave, the sheep thought hard,
And the chickens fluttered about the yard,
As each considered what to bring
As a suitable gift for the Manger's King.

The cows approached the Child's rude crib
And, proffering their tails as a kind of bib,
They fed Him butter, milk, and cheese
Sweet as the combs of honeybees.   64

The sheep presented their wooly fleece;
An ox produced some axle-grease;
And reverently twelve hens prayed
He would accept the eggs they'd laid.

Now in the rafters all this while
A snake looked on, and seemed to smile.
"What fools," it thought, "these poultry be.
Their eggs aren't fit for such as He.   72

"He is a King, and Kings are fed
On better fare than in barns is bred.
I know of eggs that Kings would kill for—
So let me slither there and pilfer!"

Then down a hanging rope it slid
As liquidly as any squid;
Through wilderness it wound its way
To a pelican's nest all daubed with clay,   80

And there by stealth it found its treasure:
An Egg whose very shape spelled Pleasure.
"Oh, how the Child will relish this!"
And it took up the Egg in a kind of kiss.

The snake returned with self-applause,
The Egg secure within its jaws,
But when it reached the Star-lit stable
To give its gift, it wasn't able!   88

For while the snake had stopped and rested
The pelican's Egg had been digested,
And all it could give was the broken shell.
"God send," it hissed, "all fowl to Hell!"

"A snake!" the Lady screamed. "A snake!
Joseph, kill it, for Heaven's sake!"
"Now, Mary dear, don't be upset:
The thing's behaving like a pet."   96

"Crush it! Smash it! Drive it away!
To think I've lived to see the day
When snakes should curl about the head
Of our dear Jesus in his bed."

Her spouse obediently shooed
The serpent off, and a somber mood
Settled upon the pilgrim throng,
Who thought that *they'd* done something wrong.   104

"My dear friends, cock-a-doodle-doo!"
The rooster addressed the little zoo.
"Every creature tame or wild
Must get a present for that Child.

"See how his fingers grasp the air
For Christmas gifts that are not there.
Go! Find new sources of Delight
And bring them back while still it's night."   112

Then, like a swarm of anxious shoppers,
Wherein rich men and ragged paupers
Mingle with but a single purpose,
Loaded with presents like Indian Sherpas,

The animals poured into the streets
With worried mews and nervous bleats.
What to get Him? Where to look?
Was He too young for a shepherd's crook?   120

The stores were closed, for it was late,
And the animals got in a terrible state,
Until the dog spoke up. "I know!
Together we'll stage a variety show!"

"What a fine idea," said the crow.
"I've sung in France as M. Corbeau
With Reynard here as accompanist."
"He sings," winked the fox, "like a soloist."   128

"Good!" said the dog. "Let's go and rehearse.
I'll write a monologue in verse
By way of setting the proper tone,
Then if we've time I'll look for a bone."

An hour later the show was ready
(Though the crow's voice was a bit unsteady),
So back to the manger the animals filed
To present their show to the sleepy Child.   136

The dog declaimed a little speech:
"Lord of the World, we here beseech,
Et cetera." And then the crow
Did its rendition of "Old Black Joe,"

Which Joseph enjoyed but Mary said
Was over Baby Jesus's head.
"For look, my dear, he's nodding off
There where he lies in the feeding trough."   144

But the show went on. "From Marshy Lake—
Lady and Gentleman—it's Duck and Drake,
To give you their impression of
A famous pair of geese in love."

The ducks quacked loud, the ducks quacked long,
And their jokes convulsed the pilgrim throng.
Mary whispered for Joseph to stoop:
"All I can think of is hot duck soup."   152

The ducks decamped; the dog returned,
Beaming with pride at the laughs they'd earned.
"May I have your attention, please,
For Puff and her Performing Fleas!"

Joseph needed no more than that.
He waved a broom at the mangey cat.
"Now, scat!" he shouted at her. "Scram!"
We won't have fleas on the little Lamb."   160

"Thank you, dear," his wife said later
"I'd had enough of their theater.
Cats are one thing; fleas another.
I'm not alone. Ask any mother."

In the silence that ensued
The animals felt a strange new mood
Waft through the manger like a wind
Bearing blossoms of tamarind,   168

And as they felt that wind to sweep
The tired animals fell asleep.
The fox and the dog, the hens and sheep
Snuggled together all of a heap.

The Wise Men to their tents retired.
"Excuse us, please. We're very tired."
"And so are we," the Lady said.
"It's time we all got into bed."   176

Starlight glinted on new-fallen snow,
And from on high a Voice sang low:
"Sleep now, my sheep, in heavenly peace,
And sleep Thou, too, My Masterpiece."

While all slept soundly in the manger,
Elsewhere a child was in great danger—
For see: the serpent seems to grin
At the infant daughter of the Inn.   184

The innocent dreamed in her trundle bed
As the snake lay coiled on the woolen spread,
And what she dreamed we'll never know,
But the wily snake reflected so:

"It's just as I remembered it:
There in the hand of this little chit,
That hollow gourd. I've seen her shake it
Hours on end. Now will I take it—   192

"But no! There may be gourds much finer
In the field in back of the Bethlehem Diner.
I'll go there now and take the best
To lay upon His sleeping breast,

"And like this girl He'll laugh and prattle
And want to *thank* me for His rattle,
And as His best friend He'll have me
And none of these curs of Galilee."   200

Then to the wintry field it slunk,
And over a wall by a dead tree trunk,
To choose from the Yuletide season's hoard
A single perfect hollow gourd.

Then back the way that it had come
To the sound of its internal drum,
Until it came to the slumbering manger
And lay before the little Stranger.   208

From the Red Sea to the Baltic
There is an action peristaltic
By which one swallows what one chews,
And whether we're snakes or cockatoos

It can't be stopped once it has started,
And so the snake was broken-hearted,
Because its gourd, its Holy Grail,
For Baby Jesus was—in its tail!   216

Its disappointment turned to rage,
And serpent nature took center stage.
"If I can't achieve another thing,
There's one surprise I still can spring."

It coiled itself in a knot of spite.
"Let *this* help you to sleep tonight
Beneath the cold snow's deepest drift!"
And it spread its jaws to give its Gift.   224

Its evil intent so thrilled the snake
That its swollen tail began to shake,
And at the sound of the hollow gourd
The Child awoke (though His folks still snored)

And clapped His infant hands with glee
And snapped the snakeskin rattle free.
"Why, thank you, Snake. Is this for Me?
Come here and sit upon my knee   232

"And let me stroke each shining scale
And help regenerate your tail."
The snake complied with snakish blushes
And joined the Child in His bed of rushes.

"*Your* gift, bright Snake, was dearest of all—
Not just your brutish wherewithal,
But something to suit a baby's whims
Better than a hundred hymns."   240

The snake could feel its tail grow whole
And a blessed sweetness pierce its soul.
With wonderment its jaws gaped wide,
And this is what the snake replied:

"I thank you, Lord, and for Thy sake
My tambour thus I'll ever shake,
The lowliest being in Thy choir.
And now, dear Lord, let me expire."   248

"My Goodness, no! The Son of Man
Needs you for His eternal plan.
Now listen to what I have in mind
For you and others of your kind.

"So man may fly as you encroach
And *you* may live above reproach,
Always before you enter battle
You'll warn your foes with this same rattle.   256

"Now go in peace. My Mother's stirring.
We don't want another scene occurring."
The serpent's tongue met the infant's lips
Like the first taste of potato chips,

And the Child knew Sin, and the snake knew Love,
And in the heavens high above
The angels sang of Peace on Earth
And the wonder of the God-Child's birth.   264

The Eightfold Way: A Masque in Five Tableaux

First Tableau

A funeral parlor. Flowers arranged about a casket. A single red gladiolus fallen to the floor.

Standing before the casket, his back to the audience, looking down at the corpse, is a man dressed in the peculiar cutaway clothes in which corpses are dressed. As the lights go up, he turns round and we see that his face is identical to that looking up from the casket.

Corpse

All right, three guesses who I am. I'll almost
Guarantee you've heard of me, assuming
You read the *Times*, and I don't mean just obituaries.
I'm talking Section A, page one, headlines.
Of course it's true, the minute one dies
Identity's less of an issue: who one was,
What one did, what one was paid for doing it.
The best thing about death is that it is a real
Vacation, no work or worries snuck in the luggage,
A ticket to Hawaii, an empty calendar,
A cloudless horizon. Ask any corpse his favorite color
And he will tell you, blue. The problem
With that, from a dramatic point of view
(And I'm as aware as you are that I'm on this stage—
Or page, as the case may be—and cannot otherwise
Than as a figure of fiction communicate with you:
C'est la mort!), the problem with such a Polynesian
Mode of death is that a living audience
Has little incentive to tune in.

The lovelier the weather we report, the more
We wish you were here, the fewer our listeners.
Only bad news sells newspapers, the latest scoop from—

*A large mechanical mouse runs across the stage, spins
around, and disappears under the casket.*

Corpse
[*after a moment's alarm*]
Hell! Now, there's an example of what I mean:
Rats, and rotting in a coffin, and all the other
Gothic traditions connected with death.
It's worse than fraternities and hazings,
A bigger disgrace than Edwin Meese.
Mice! Rats! Maggots and centipedes!
Even for a disembodied spirit like myself
The mind shrinks from such images, but for you
Who are still organic, how dreadful to think
Of lips and eyeballs and other delicate tissues
Becoming carrion. Embalming is supposed
To help: scavengers take one whiff and scurry off
To meats that have been curried with other spices.
Well, whether rats eat it or not, flesh
Will rot, and the thought's disquieting.
Even now, a corpse, I'd rather think of myself
As a statue than as a side of pickled beef.
Though even with stone there's some attrition.
Just this year a new hunk of the Sphinx
Broke off. But even so, for the long haul
Across the millennia, basalt must beat
Formaldehyde, or even aluminum siding.

*The mechanical Mouse re-enters and listens to the Corpse with a skep-
tical smile. He has grown to human size and is dressed in cheery
summer clothes. He's carrying a plastic shopping bag supplied with
various props.*

*The Corpse continues to address the audience, unaware yet of the
Mouse.*

Corpse

I've yet to tell you who I am, or was.
Want a hint? Think of the word "shrink."
Think of the social sciences. Not anthropology.
Not soc—

Mouse

                    [*playfully*]
                              Perhaps religion? Were you
Some great Divine?

Corpse

                              In fact, I'm not at all
Religious.
        [*turns, sees the Mouse, shrieks*]
                    O Jesus, no! O Christ!

Mouse

I didn't mean to interrupt. Continue:
You were playing guessing games, and threw "shrink"
Out as a clue. Could it be your surname's Fink?

Corpse

        [*offended*]
Could it be *your* first name's Mickey?

Mouse

Please don't suggest that, even as a jest!
The Disney people can be fearfully litigious.
I would be off this stage and out of print
In minutes, if they suspected I were not
Generically the merest *mus domesticus*.
Besides, have I his voice, his mien, his air
Of innocence, his sweet neoteny?
I more resemble you, or Marilyn Monroe,
Than Mickey Mouse. Now to the business
(We'll say no more of cartoon animals)
Of your afterlife. How would you like to be
Brought back? Animal, mineral, or (re-in)carnation?

Corpse

I've only just popped off. Why can't I poke
About eternity a while, meet God, enjoy my reward?

Mouse

Cheese?

Corpse

                Beg pardon?

Mouse

                        Some milk in decay?
Let's see: there's Camembert, Muenster,
A rather stiff Brie. And sliced Velveeta.

Corpse

Even in the afterlife?

Mouse

                        "On earth as it is
In heaven" works both ways. I've also got
A tolerable zinfandel. The newly dead
Tend to be thirsty.

Corpse
[*as the Mouse uncorks the bottle and lays out a lunch on top of
the casket*]
                Well, I am fond
Of Camembert, and I always did like plays
Where people ate real food on stage
And drank real liquor. Though it's only the beer
You can believe, when the can is popped
And it comes frothing out. Anything else
Is too easily faked. Vodka's obviously water,
But even a bottle that seems to have been corked—
        [*The Mouse pops the cork of the wine bottle and pours out two
        glasses.*]
Might prove to be grape juice, or just—

[*They toast and drink*]

                                            —water
With coloring added. I'm disappointed.

Mouse

The wine is real enough. It's *you* who've lost
Your sense of taste, and smell, and all the rest.
For all your lifeless tongue could tell
You might have drunk your own exsanguinated blood
And not an '87 Napa Valley zinfandel.

Corpse

Heaven, it seems, leaves much to be desired.

Mouse

Those were the very words of Tantalus.
If you'd enjoy the pleasures you are used to,
You'll have to be reborn. The process can be
Slow as rusting, for first you must be disassembled
To a subatomic state, letting the elements
Of self flake away like paint, until you're
Simplified into a single quintessential quark.
It's taken some Pharaohs until this century
To shrink until they've fit the flesh of housewives
In the suburbs of Phoenix, Arizona.
But I know a quicker way.

Corpse

                                To make me a Phoenix
Hausfrau?

Mouse

                        Or less, or more. You *won't* be
What you were before, that's the only guarantee.
A potted ginko, possibly; a crab, a crane,
A little bitty baby with no brain.
All things are possible in *this* hereafter
Except for grief, or reverence, or laughter.
The microuniverse in which I'll be your cicerone

16

Exists without respect for human feelings.
Indifference is beauty, and beauty's truth:
That's all you need to know.

Corpse

If I'm to play

Dante to your Virgil, I'll have to know
A little more than that.

Mouse
Add this then:
Death can be embarrassing. You must undress.
   [*responding to the Corpse's gestures of threatened modesty*]
Oh, it's not your rotting flesh you must expose.
You must shrug off your name, your history,
Your pride. All you believed must be denied
And all you loathed accepted.

Corpse
My name, my name . . . It's already gone,
But not the names I used to drop: Johnson,
Jackson, Jacobs, Michaels, Miller, Moore.
I knew them all, and dined with one or two.
I sent them Christmas cards and signed them
With my name, my name . . . which has evaporated!

Mouse
For now that's a sufficient sacrifice
To admit you to the first sub-level
Of your disassemblage. It's through that door.

Corpse
I see no door.

The coffin at center stage rotates ninety degrees and revolves so that the Corpse is standing face to face with the embalmed body in the coffin.

Second Tableau

The light quivers. The Corpse tentatively places his hand on the doorknob of the coffin. There is a rumbling sound, as of a vault opening. A blackout. A sudden blast of perfume. When the lights come on, the Corpse and the Mouse have shrunk down to insect size, so that the entire set behind them is felled with the petals of the red gladiolus that lay on the floor beside the casket.

Corpse

Now I remember who you are! Sniffles!
Of the comic-book team of Mary-Jane and Sniffles.
When I was little, I would go out behind the house,
Scrunch down by an anthill and pretend to be her,
Reciting her magic rhyme: "Puff, puff, piffles,
Make me just as small as Sniffles," and she would shrink
To Sniffles' size, this size, mouse size, and off they'd go
Adventuring in a world where any garbage can
Could become a cathedral.

Mouse

We're mouse-size now, that much is so,
But no, I'm not Sniffles, and if I were,
It would not be very kind of you to blow
My incognito. Copyright, copyright!
Next you'll insist that I am plagiarizing
Fantastic Voyage.

Corpse

Right, I remember it!

That's the one about a team of doctors
Who travel in a teeny-tiny submarine
Along the bloodstream of their patient.
Lord, that takes me back: Nineteen-Sixty-Six!
I would have been. . . . Now that's gone, too,
Along with every other memory of being young.

Mouse

And look how much lovelier the world's become
As a result. Without a past specific to yourself
There is no guilt winding up your nerves
Like an alarm clock, no pre-set agenda to say
Now do this, now do that. You are free
To contemplate a flower for an hour at a time.

Corpse

[*contemplating the vast petals of the set glumly*]
Yes, if I were so inclined. But flowers
Only put me in mind of sickbeds and biers.
If I were a bee, I'd see things differently
No doubt.

Mouse

You might become a bee.

Corpse

Bing Crosby sang a song to that effect
In some movie where he was a priest,
A song about reincarnation.
   [*hums melody of "Aren't You Glad You're You?"*]
No, I don't think I'd like to be reborn
A bee.

Mouse

You're avoiding the issue,
Which is the power that a flower can exercise
Over our imaginations.

Corpse

An *hour*
Tickling my nose with a rose? I'd die.

Mouse

With the ghost of a rose. Why don't you try?

The Mouse reaches into his bag and takes out a baton. With his back to the audience, he conducts the Weber-Berlioz "Invitation to the Dance." As the Corpse is caught up by the music, dancing with increasing energy, the Mouse offers a voice-over narration.

Mouse

You are waking from a dream, a young girl
Home from your first ball, and your pretty head
Tinkles and glows like a crystal chandelier!
Once again the remembered waltz whirls
You through space like a satellite of tulle and lace.

The Corpse, waltzing, plucks one of the petals of the giant gladiolus and wraps it round himself, capelike, exposing, as he does so, a door at the flower's center. The door opens and from it Nijinsky, in his costume as the Spectre of the Rose, leaps onto the stage to join the Corpse in his ever more impassioned dance.

Mouse

And then—O can your maiden heart sustain
Such joy!—and then—O heavens, can it be?—
It is he! The ghost of the rose you wore at the ball,
Whose breath is a breeze freighted with fragrances
Of Chanel! of Guerlain! of Cacharel and Giorgio Armani!
Whose touch is the caress of thousand-dollar bills
Drifting like soot from the chimneys of Paradise.
He whispers to you, he begs to repose on your breast
As on the tomb incised with his name—Nijinsky!

The naming of the Spectre should coincide with the high point of the music and with the very quick substitution of the actor playing the Corpse—wrapped in the gladiolus petal, whirling into the wings and quickly back again—by his female counterpart, who is dressed, like Nijinsky, in the costume traditionally worn by ballerinas in this role. Gladys (as the Corpse's female counterpart will be called) and Nijinsky perform again, with great artistry, a passage of their pas de deux that had been less ably executed when the Corpse had been dancing with Nijinsky.

20

As the music comes to an end, Nijinsky sweeps up Gladys and bears her off through the gladiolus's door.

Third Tableau

The set represents a part of a complex protein molecule that extends beyond the stage in all directions. It is formed of aluminum rods, inflated beach balls, neon lights, steel girders, and panels of Mylar. From time to time elements within the protein molecule shift position or vibrate. A variety of humming sounds swell and ebb in conjunction with a barely perceptible strobing of the light. Gladys and Nijinsky are seated on the molecule, eating yogurt from paper cups.

Gladys

I have this image of myself on a golden throne
Surrounded by a multitude of worshippers,
But whether they're worshipping me or I'm only
A sort of high priestess I can't be sure.
It isn't even clear that I'm a woman, I might be a man.
Perhaps one of the Pharaohs of ancient Egypt,
Wouldn't *that* be amazing? That's why
I'm a vegetarian, you see. Because if we do
Have other lives than this, if we return
In other forms, who's to say we're necessarily
Human each time around? You might have been a cat,
For instance, that would explain your *tours en l'air.*

Nijinsky

Why is it women seem unable to *think?*
Is it genetic, or does their casual acceptance
Of fantasy as fact spring from having played
With dolls, while boys are drilled in a quick grasp
Of vector quantities?

Gladys

                         Oh, Vaslav, please—

Not math.

Nijinsky

There, you're doing it,

Acting the role of the gold-digging ditz
Too dumb to number the rings on her fingers
And bells on her toes.

Gladys

I liked you better

When you were a rose.

Nijinsky

It's not as though

Dancers were exempted from the laws
That govern the collisions of planets
And of molecules. Look, when I pirouette,
Then draw my leg closer to my torso, so,
My spin picks up speed. Physics and math
Are not arcane. The wisdom of Euclid
And Pythagoras is carved into the calcium
Of our bones, welded to the iron of our blood.

Gladys

Then there must be another level of being,
Larger than planets or smaller than molecules,
Where the soul may go, as to a dressing room,
To change the clothing of its flesh. Ballet
Is not, not, not about our physicality.
Ballet is love! When you kiss me,
Surely you aren't thinking what a nice piece
Of meat you have in your mouth, how much
More succulent than sirloin.

Nijinsky

Let us

Put it to the test.

Gladys

Vaslav! Be serious!

Nijinsky kisses Gladys passionately. Music from Wagner's Tristan.

Nijinsky

Adenine!

Gladys
Guanine!

Nijinsky
Inevitable.

Gladys
Interlinking.

Nijinsky

O sugary necessity.

Gladys
Fated attraction.
We that were, apart, mere purposeless proteins
Become, united, a nucleotide,
Latest links of a millennial chain
That binds us twain to the sun-stirred tides
Of the primal ocean, eternal bouillabaisse,
Parentless parent, patient, procreative
Source of all that hungers and seeks
To connect.

Nijinsky
Dearest double-ringed purine!
Adulated adenine! You are the socket!
I am the plug!

Gladys
These are my fingers!
This is their glove! I slip into the groove
Necessity has smoothed for me, and my skin
Is soothed by a breeze of spring. Yin
Meets her Yang.

Nijinsky
                          Sturm meets his Drang.

Both
Bonded together, never to part,
Guanine to adenine, as Camus to Sartre.
Each alone issueless, together the source
Of infinite progeny, love and remorse.

A bell knells.

Brangäne
  [*offstage*]
You two had better simmer down.
Proteins disintegrate as proteins grow.
Molecules come and molecules go,
And love is part of the passing show.

Nijinsky
Cytosine!

Gladys
Thymine!

Nijinsky
                          Sight unseen . . .

Gladys
                          Thine is mine!

Nijinsky
A pyrimidine paragon.

Gladys
                    What care I where I am
While I am with you? Were you of uracil,
Still would I love you, still would my oxygen
Lock to your phosphorus. Across the Aegean

And up through the Bosporus, my galley should sail,
Like a new Cleopatra's.

Nijinsky

                              Nuclear energies
Fuel our desire! Fissioning nuclei
Shine from your eyes. Radiant Cytosine!

Gladys
Thymine, my other self! Mythical twin,
Twining with me in serpentine helices,
Mirror reversing right and left,
Machine of perpetual emotion,
Loom on which the shuttles of my soul
Flash to and fro, genetic spinning jenny,
Sin with me, spin with me
Deoxyribonucleically.

A bell knells. The Mouse enters from stage left.

Mouse
Well, *someone's* feeling her Cheerios!
I hate to be a party pooper, but that bell's tolling
For you. It's time to wind on down the road.

Gladys
I'm staying with Vaslav! You'll never move me!
As long as I have life and breath—

Mouse
But you have neither: had you forgot?
I'll tell you what, I'll help you change
Your mind as easily as shifting gears.
Just step over by these smoking mirrors. . . .

Gladys allows herself to be led before the largest Mylar panel.

Gladys
There's no reflection.

Mouse
                                        Because these mirrors
Reveal the voids and vacancies
Interleaving our lives. In death
Matter matters less and less, as breath
By breath our flesh is sublimated into air,
And that air itself is rarefied to ether.
Here all the zeroes of Arabia
Glisten like dew-sequined blossoms
On the tree of night. *Capisce?*

Gladys
Not a word. Indeed, while you've been speaking,
I think I've disappeared.

Mouse
                                        No, only grown
Smaller, diminishing to your atomic height.
I'll follow you at *c*, the speed of light!

*The Mouse steps through the Mylar panel, from which there issues
a blinding burst of light.*

Fourth Tableau

*The nucleus of an atom, composed of large inflated balloons, on which
the Corpse and the Mouse recline, as on a hemispherical waterbed.
From time to time an electron speeds through the enveloping darkness
in the form of a television monitor. The Corpse has reverted to his
original male format.*

Corpse
   [*sings*]
Suppose the West's declined already.
Suppose the gathered rose is sick,
The cupboard bare, the limbs unsteady
That once were capable and quick.

Yet still will positrons obey
Nature's eternal protocols,
The same tomorrow as they are today
For atoms as for basketballs.

Still will swift electrons spin
In faery rings about their nuclei,
Their beauty intrinsic and not in
Any beholder's beholding eye.

Do not mourn, therefore, the loss
Of a planet's cast-off clothes.
History's a coverlet of moss
To mantle drunkards' oaths.

Mouse

Here in the so much simpler realm
Of subatomic particles, we have arrived
At the Jerusalem foretold by the prophets
From Paul to Nietzsche, a *Götterdämmerung*
Without wrong or right, where light's not polarized
In days and nights, but restless vacillates
In troughs and crests. Here the tangled yarn
Of history becomes as clear a tale
As that of Oedipus or Peter Rabbit,
No labyrinth but a simple repeating
Greek-key motif along the hem
Of the millennium. Shall I unfold
A mystery? Then listen as electrons speak!

Electron

[*appearing as a talking head in the TV that flies by above the
atom's nucleus*]
Half-lives had we who ran half-hearted-
Or unmindfully the race that's to be run
Against time's tireless tortoises.
Neglecting our principia, obeying venal
Princes, we died before we could be senile,

And though still we seemed to live,
We had decayed from radium to lead.

Corpse

Was that really *Achilles* on TV?

Mouse

One cannot say of any electron that it is
Precisely anyone at any given moment.
Like our imaginations, or good actors,
Their identities are liquid. See,
Already it has changed channels.

Electron

[*a new head on the screen*]
Brighter and brighter, the fat's in the fire,
The bombs fall down, and masses expire:
Mere anarchy is loosed upon the world.

Tighter and tighter, the knot of the wire's
Secured by the fingers of Einstein and Teller,
While down in the cellar the wine turns to blood.

Wave and particle, particle and wave,
Let who can save himself himself now save.
To the rest best regards and an unmarked grave.

Corpse

If I were larger than I have become, as big
As a gene or a gnat, I might be moved by such
Knelling of the bell of nuclear doom. But now
I'm *not* for whom that bell tolls. I'm free
Of all Befores and Afters. Where's my remote?
  [*aims bleeper at TV*]
No more *News of the World*! I cast my vote
For *Death-Styles of the Rich and Famous*!

Electron

[*a new head, speaking in the accents of Robin Leach*]

Welcome, particles one and all,
To the odd environs of Heisenberg Hall.
Built at simply staggering expense,
Defying reason and confounding sense,
This masterpiece of mathematics
Has seven million meta-attics
Each equipped with a cloud chamber and a bath
Designed according to the highest math.
So *chic* is it, so *très exquise*,
Eye cannot see it, nor can hand squeeze,
For if a single particle of light
Should strike its turrets, it would take flight,
And before you've said, "I think it's there,"
It would be off, you'd know not where.
Thus to the naked human eye
Heisenberg Hall is only fence and sky,
A vision of what might have been
If hand could touch what to the eye's unseen.

Corpse

How beautiful! How new! In such a house
I'd be content to be the merest mouse.
No slight intended.

Mouse

And none taken.
Are you all right? You do seem shaken.

Corpse

For a moment there I thought I saw
A glint, a flicker, a flash, a hint
Of something curiously like . . . me!
But of such strangeness and such charm—

A buzzer sounds twice, and two birds bearing placards saying "Strangeness" and "Charm" come down on wires, after the manner of You Bet Your Life.

Mouse

The secret words!

Corpse

                                         And secret worlds

Are opened to our view.

Mouse

                                         This atom, too.

The nucleus splits, and its constituent balloons bounce off into the wings and out into the audience. The Corpse and the Mouse exit via a trapdoor beneath the splitting atom.

Fifth Tableau

A void. Very quiet music from a gamelan orchestra. The allegorical figures of Strangeness (the Corpse in a white robe) and Charm (the Mouse, unmasked and dressed for tennis) enter, and address the audience antiphonally.

Strangeness and Charm

Strangeness am I.

                                         And I'm charm.

Together we embody

                                         Something that cannot exist

But does: heads

                                         Without tails, spin

Without mass, either

                                         Without an or,

After *sans* before.

Strangeness

All that heretofore has seemed mysterious
We'll now be able to explain.

Charm

To wit: he's daft, and I'm delirious.

Strangeness regards Charm reproachfully.

Charm
I'm sorry. I see we must be serious.

Strangeness
  [hieratically]
Quantum and Qabbalah together comprise
The high Platonic propylaeum
To what our physicists denominate
The Eightfold Way, whereon
One melds in Three, and Three's subsumed in Two,
And every Number finds its proper Form,
A snowflake in the heavens' systematic storm.

Charm
Or dewdrop (the comparison's as apt)
Fallen on a daisy's lenient lap.
We count the petals: *loves me . . . loves me* not . . .
Baryon and burial, hadron and hard-on,
Each one congruent with a thought
In the all-connecting mind of Murray Gell-Mann,
Time's last cosmogonist, atomic Dante.
Welcome, Strangeness, to his game of three-shell monte.

  [revealing a cardboard with three shells on it, which he begins
    rapidly to slide about]
Beneath one shell's the small green pea
Inscribed with your next identity.
Beneath the other two is *niente,*
Nothing, *nada, Nichts, rien.*
This one? Or this? Or this? Say when.

*Strangeness points to one of the shells. Charm lifts it. The lights flare
to their brightest and then go black.*

1 2 3 4

Back Here

The buildings they were tearing down
The last time I was in this town
Have been replaced by parking lots,
And every friend conceals his thoughts.

For instance, that my eyes have grown
Remoter than the eyes he'd known.
We talk about the way that Time's
Rewarded us for all our crimes.

Garage Sale

Once someone thought he'd want to read this book,
And here's a chess set minus just one rook;
A Sunbeam toaster sans its cord; the *Life*
Of Who's-It by his unforgiving wife.
Como singing "Dance, Ballerina, Dance";
The buttons off a hundred shirts and pants;
A rug unfaded where a bed had been
With traffic patterns marked in olive green.
There are few takers, though the prices cry,
"Remember, stranger, someday you must die."

A Questionnaire

My mother is in heaven now
   (A year ago she died):
If I were still eleven, how
   Long would I have cried?

Say I left home at seventeen
   (When she was thirty-five):
Tell me—how old would she have been
   Today, were she alive?

Mother in heaven, look at me!
   (I'm wiggling my ears!)
Can you still hear, and can you see
   My giggling, my tears?

On Depositing the Check for a Legacy

Dinner is over and not much is left—
Bones that might contribute to a soup,
Some sticks of celery, and two burnt tarts.

Into the icebox with it all. Sweep off
The crumbs and leave the dishes in the sink.
Let's open the brandy and play hearts.

To an Elder Brother, Aborted

I never feel myself alone
In caves or in abandoned houses.
Back in the darkness, behind a door,
I expect to find you scraping
Some bare subsistence, tearing up the floors
For firewood, asleep in piss,
In a state of glorious neglect,
Or murdered, quite mysteriously.
I've waited long enough, God knows,
To hear your version of the years
I missed, to sift the evidence
And rehearse the time between your arrival
And mine. In bars and empty buses,
On dark streets, I've introduced myself
To you, and you would stand and stare—
But was it *me* who wasn't there?
We need each other, for alone
Our alibis will not make sense.
Brother, believe me—it wasn't I
Who turned the lights off and made you cry.

The Friends of Long Ago

Unwelcome guests come earliest.
They linger in the kitchen, hungry
For confidences. Their glasses
Unerringly light on the best wood.
Shameless as the wine they bring,
They praise the food their presence turns
To carrion. Their kisses are carcinogens.
Only the eyes, trapped in their ruins,
Bear witness to the appetites and lies
Once so ungrudgingly shared.
Be resolute: ask after their torments—
The novel abandoned, the ex-wife, the diet.
When at last they leave, do not
Let them forget their umbrellas.

Old Friends

As their inked or pencilled names
Calmly disintegrate; as the spaces
Of their various rented rooms condense
Into a single spartan ugliness;
As any feelings for them are dispersed
Into the city's wide chattering
Nights, all but these dry branches
Of a handshake (which, stranger,
I am not offering to you); as I sift
This morning through the Troys
Of five, ten, fifteen years ago,
The tawdry gifts too carefully exchanged,
Preserved by chance or parsimony
And now displayed to represent,
Deservedly, my life and character;
As I, unwitnessing, walk by them
In all their awful dailiness—
They laugh at me, knowing,
As I do not, who next
Among the friends I think I still possess
Will let it slip, the secret we all share
Who have been friends too long.

My Willoughby Personality Schedule

(abridged)

Sometimes I worry about humiliating experiences
but when there is no real danger of falling I am not afraid
Often my feelings are easily hurt, as often as not
I keep in the background at social events.

Sometimes I'm happy and sad by turns without knowing why
but I'm not *very* shy
Often I daydream, as often as not
I like to be alone.

Sometimes I am easily discouraged
but I don't mind it when people watch me work
Often I'm lonely, as often as not
when I see an accident something keeps me from giving help.

Who am I?

The Self as Product

Though you may consider it an undesirable
Property, rest assured that somewhere
Its purchaser exists and is looking
For something exactly like you.
Keep placing ads. Rehearse your smile.
Go everywhere you're invited, and polish
Your best anecdotes like family silver.
If nothing happens, reassess
Your asking price or change agencies.
Above all, seem to enjoy yourself.
People need to see the product used.

How to Identify Yourself in a Crowd

You are the one who looks like that:
You wear a suit, a tie, a hat.

Or else (supposing him too fat)
You are that *other* bureaucrat

With skin of bronze and stomach flat
And whiskers from the Rubaiyat:

In all the race there's not a rat
Who doesn't think you're where it's at.

But bear in mind this caveat:
You're only protein to a cat.

A Call to Lost Members

Return, *amici*, to the monthly meeting,
Or soon the Secretary's stern, deleting
Ballpoint shall strike your name from every list.
Rejoin us now while yet your voice is missed
And your advances give us cause to wonder.
The younger lions who would steal your thunder
Already prowl the velvet-curtained lounge,
As quick to vilify a friend as scrounge
A cigarette from your old editor.
Be present, *entre nous*, as predator
Or, if you *will* extend your holiday,
Your name and novels are predestined prey.
Prove by a letter, at the very least,
That though you're absent you have not deceased.

To Fame

My darling, come! Caress me! Tear me limb
From limb, and make my heart the souvenir
Of any oaf who's taken by the whim
To tear it out of me. Let me appear
On *Time*, my dear, and make John Simon praise
What he has utterly misunderstood.
Exalt my foibles into fads, amaze
My friends, and let my sales be all they should.
Repeat my name and tell of my success
Till everyone is sick of me. Oh, pass beyond
A mere satiety to gross excess
So that I may eclipse the whole beau monde.
At last, when I am dead, my lovely, please
To auction off my corpse at Sotheby's.

Sunday at Home

There is someone in a chair, just there,
Reading, and in an adjoining room
Light bulbs incandesce against a gloom
Of shelves and boxes. I do not know where
I am, unless I am with you. I share
The silence of the afternoon with whom
I can: with you, if you are there. The doom
Of private life's just possible to bear
Until the light permits a glass of wine,
Until the flicker of the Evening News
Resumes its homilies of yours and mine,
Of strengths and shortages, until we lose
Our sense of ingrown singleness and dine
Alone and yet together, as we choose.

So Grows the Tree

It is at the very tips of the branches,
where the bending twigs discuss
their future goals, it is at the tips
of the branches, where roles are first adopted,
whether to grow north or south or whether to grow
at all, it is there at the tips
of the twigs, among the children counting
their birthdays with a furious wish
to be older and free, it is there
at the tips of the branches that the rose will appear.

What's *Left Unsaid, or* The Dodo's Joy

Does the chipmunk whom we fed
Remember us in his warm bed?
As he sleeps, do we recur
In rodent dream, the way we were,
Begging him to take the alms
Extended in well-meaning palms?

Did the cardinals in their nest
Consider us a kind of pest,
Related to the seeds they ate
But, even so, a sorry fate,
Accepted as a fate must be
Because of dire necessity?

I can't believe love is so blind:
However minuscule the mind
That hesitates before the seeds
Another offers to its needs,
The moment of acceptance brings
A sense of joy to toes or wings—

Not the slaking of a thirst,
But what the Dodo felt when first
Adam offered it a name,
And so a share in all the fame
That comes of being born on Earth
And knowing God and having worth.

A Tree in the Dark

Yes of course
the caterpillars have been here
eating us   I knew that
simple fact
long before you noticed
But I don't dwell on it
If they return
next year in force
as they well may
some of us will die
But might not you
from causes
no less inexorable
Which is not to say
that we are fatalists
Only trees among other trees
who tonight enjoy
whatever breezes
the season offers
So should you
Let the daily
reoccurrence of the light
be your sufficient
parable   What is one year
more or less
Think of the poor mushrooms
and take heart
What have they
to look forward to

Spores and more
spores   We have
enjoyed our lifetimes
Cheer up   The sun also
surprises

Why This Tie, Why That

Because it has class,
because it accords with our common sense
        of a relationship
        only lately perceived
        between this gray and these greens
        named not two years ago by the Federal Council
                on Color;
Because we are all slightly tired
        of yesterday's answer to the riddle posed
        by the face in the mirror
        (and anyhow this is not the same shirt), and
because this tie is like a rich dessert, a promising
        yet unassertive brown suggestive of Kahlua.

Because it was foremost on the rack (or farthest back),
because X wore one just like it
        with undeniable panache;
because I'm in the throes of love
        and love is like a red red rose.

Because I'm blue.

Because I can recall the very moment there
        in Hung on You so long ago
        when I thought: yes, this tie
        is an entire Hawaiian shirt
        condensed into one dazzling rhombus!

Because you gave it to me, or maybe
because I gave it you (in error).

Because we're in France, or, likelier,
because we wish we were;
because most people would never dare to wear it, and, equally,
because they would, and
because this is exactly who I am,
        could be, might wish to be,
        today, this afternoon, or some day soon.

1 2 3 4

The Joycelin Shrager Story

When people asked what he did, Donald Long's standard riposte was, "I'm a mechanic of the dream." Meaning, he was a projectionist. Actually, few people had to ask, since Donald had been around since the first black-and-white flickerings of the Movement early in the fifties. With the money he earned at the Europa he produced *Footage*, first as a quarterly and then a bi-monthly. For years it was their only magazine, but gradually, as success changed the Movement into the Underground, *Footage* was supplemented and then supplanted by newer, more commercially oriented magazines. Donald Long's reputation as the Rhadamanthus of the underground film was undiminished, and possibly enhanced, by reason of this failure, but there was one consequence to be regretted—he had to continue full-time at the Europa, from one in the afternoon till the early evening, six days a week, in order to support his magazine and himself.

The Europa is on 8th Avenue, just below 49th. Originally it had been a showcase for Russian, Polish, and Estonian movies not otherwise distributed in the city, but then, imperceptibly, without a change of owner (or, so far as Donald could see, of clientele), the Europa drifted toward a policy of nudism and the exposure of organized vice, especially the white slavery traffic. By the end of '69, the Sexual Revolution had swept the October Revolution into oblivion.

Something of the same thing had been happening in his own life. Donald was forty-two, and after decades of honest homeliness he was finally coming into his own. What had been even ten years ago a bony kind of face was now rather striking in a severe way. No longer did he dissemble his baldness with a few iron-gray strands brushed up from the sides. No, he let it declare itself, and what hair still was left to him he grew, boldly, down to his shoulders. But best of all his somatype had become trendy, and he was able to fit into all the skimpy pullovers and striped pants that most men couldn't have attempted after the age of thirty.

Not that he became a satyr quite. He simply began taking advantage of the opportunities that had always offered themselves to him from time to time. At parties he was less diffident. He would even dance. (He had gone to a Reichian therapist and redirected some of his energies from his head down to his balls and, concomitantly, his feet.) He got rolfed, and laid.

But he didn't fall in love. He kept waiting, alert as a seismograph, for some tremor of affection, warmth, whatever. All he ever felt was a great glow of health and, toward his partners, benevolence, a degree of gratitude, a lesser degree of curiosity. But love? Never.

He knew what love was. Twice before he'd been in love. The first time, at twenty-one, he'd made the mistake of marrying his love-object, the black actress Cerise Miles. That was 1949, the year of Kazan's *Pinky*, and among enlightened Manhattanites love conquered all. By 1951 Donald and Cerise had come to hate each other much more passionately than they'd ever loved. As a result, his memories of the early, positive period of the relationship resembled, in its deliberate fuzziness, the one film Donald himself had ever made, *Tides of the Blood*. Among much else, *Tides* was a record of his marriage's collapse. (And, by implication, of Western civilization's.) Cerise had played herself, improvisationally, a performance that, even after Donald's editing, was considered a limit-case of what underground cinema could do along the lines of honesty.

The second time he was luckier and fell in love with the wife of his best friend, Gary Webb. The necessity of concealment kept Donald and Grace Webb in a state of zesty suspense and made their few rare moments alone together lyrical in the extreme. Then, after the adultery had gone on some two years, Grace felt she had to tell Gary. There was no question of divorce, since both Webbs were renegade Catholics who still believed in the sanctity of the marriage bond and the natural law. It was just her unconquerable candor. Gary was wretched and furious by turns, and Donald and Grace were rapturously guilty and more in love than ever.

Gary Webb was at that time (the late fifties) the most prolific (and, according to *Footage*, the best) director in the Movement. Film for him was less an art than a religion. He was its priest, and his camera was the sacrament he carried through the world, hallowing it. He filmed everything: snowfalls, muggings, Grace in *halasana* position, trees in Washington Square, football games on Channel Five, a friend's stoned, staring iris (a shot he was sure Hitchcock had plagiarized in *Psycho*), a dripping faucet, cars on the street, and the natural births of all six of his sons. He also filmed, with Grace's connivance, representative moments of her adultery, and this footage became the basis of his most revolutionary and well-known film, *Reel 168* (1959).

The affair ended when Gary inherited his grandfather's farm in western Kansas. The Webbs moved west, with their cats and children and cameras, and in a few months Grace had been absorbed into the irrecoverable past. Years later he was to get a postcard from either Grace or Gary, he could never be sure, to which was glued a snippet from the ad for *The Great Gatsby*: "Gone is the romance that was so divine." The card showed a motel outside of Lebanon, Kansas.

On Sunday mornings, thanks to its owner, Norman Brodkey, and to the tax laws that make such transformations so profitable, the Europa became the Foundation for Free Cinema. The foundation's screening policy was egalitarian, even kindly in a careless way, mixing established old masters like Anger and Brakhage with whatever else happened along, and throwing in an occasional reel of the Europa's indigenous beavers when their directors or actors had credentials in the Movement. This policy usually guaranteed a minimum attendance of twenty-five or thirty, comprised mainly of fledgling filmmakers, their casts, and close friends.

On this particular Sunday, May 17, 1970, the foundation was showing two works by Anna Congdon: *Stigma* (1954, 48 min.) and *Dreams of Eurydice* (1967, 73 min.). As the combined running times precluded more than a token representation of films by the foundation's regular customers, as well because Miss Congdon had never ventured from her native Australia and so lacked the social leverage by which to muster the fiction of a coterie, and finally because the weather was more than ordinarily unacceptable, the turnout stopped just one short of none at all. That one was Mike Georgiadis, whose oeuvre, long since completed, shared a common mythopoeic strain with Miss Congdon's, and at whose urgings Donald had at last agreed to give the old girl her crack at America.

Mike was propped on the stainless steel ledge of the ticket booth, coughing, joking, and smoking fifteen-cent El Productos. It was an evil, evocative cough, but pardonable when you knew that Mike was dying of emphysema, had been dying of emphysema now for all of fourteen years.

They passed the rainy minutes gossiping about colleagues, the waxing and waning of their incomes, marriages, entanglements, and reputations. Mike, who was firmly established at the waning end of all scales, had a knack for interpreting any scrap of news so as to make his friends seem morons, martyrs, or, if the news were incontestably good, thieves. Donald, whose style was to be magnanimous, praised whom he could and forgave the rest. Donald's exculpations incited Mike to ever fiercer judgments, and these in turn provoked Donald to still more ingenious charities. They worked well together.

A damp, large, lardy girl in a yellow vinyl poncho with a Bolex Rex-4 pendant from her neck like some mammoth ankh had parked herself before the foundation's mimeoed schedule, which was Scotch-taped over the glassed display of stills for *Lust Party*. As she read, her mouth and eyebrows ticked an unceasing commentary of pouts, sneers, frowns, and grave suspicions. "Disturbed" was the word that came to mind.

Mike vanished into the theater.

Donald couldn't take his eyes off the girl's Bolex. Its fittings were rusty, the leather was peeling from its sides, and its carrying strap was a doubled length of twine: a camera as woebegone as the wide, wet, hungry eyes of a Keane puppy. He was smitten.

She looked at him and looked away. She scrabbled in a tie-dyed cotton satchel and brought out a dollar bill compactly folded into sixteenths. She undid the dollar regretfully and pushed it into Donald's cage.

"Has it started yet?" she asked.

"No, not yet. We've been waiting for more people to turn up."

"Then maybe you could do me a favor?" She bared her small brown teeth in a defeated smile, like a teen-age panhandler's or a Scientologist's, that no rebuff could dismay.

"Certainly," said Donald.

"I'm making a film." When he did not contradict her she went on. "And I need some footage of me coming down the street to the theater here. All you have to do is aim the camera at me and look through here." She pointed to the viewfinder, from which the eyeguard was missing. "And touch this when I say to. Otherwise it's all wound up and ready to shoot."

Donald consented to be her assistant. He came out from the ticket window and took the wounded camera in his arms.

"Be careful with it," she thought to insist, seeing that he was careful. "These things are very expensive."

Then she walked up to the corner, turned around, fussed with her poncho, squared her shoulders, and fixed her wide, meaty lips in a smile representing an irrepressible buoyancy.

"Now!" she shouted.

Through the viewfinder he watched her advancing toward him with a sinking certainty that Fate had come in at the door without knocking. He knew she was not beautiful. Indeed, her face and figure and bearing passed beyond mere homeliness into the realm of absolutes. She was sinfully ugly. Nevertheless, his whole frame was in a tremble of sexual anxiety such as no beaver had ever roused him to.

When the film had run out, she said, "You're Donald Long, aren't you?"

He admitted he was.

"Wow, that's terrific. You know, I've read every word you've ever written?"

"No kidding."

"Yeah." She nodded her head solemnly. "So this is really an important moment in my life." Then, offering her hand: "I'm Joycelin Shrager."

Joycelin's film, *The Dance of Life* (or rather, this latest installment, for *The Dance of Life* was conceived as a *film fleuve*, ever flowing on, the unexpurgated and amazing story of her life), was screened by the Foundation for Free Cinema three Sundays later. There was a good turnout. One reason was because this was an open screening, and where there is hope there is good attendance. The other reason was because Donald had been sending out signals and his friends had rallied round, as to Roncesvalles. Jesse

Aarons, a director who was making a name in porn, had come, and Ed Gardner, who reviewed sometimes for the *Voice*; Louise Hiller, the modern dancer who had rolfed Donald, and her latest boyfriend, Muhammid Kenzo, a black painter who'd had a painting in the Whitney; the Bachofens, of the Bachofen Gallery, and their son Arnold; Mike Georgiadis, Helen Emerson, and Rafe Kramer (survivors from the older, Maja Deren era of the Art Film); Lloyd Watts, the conceptual artist who'd come to doing street signs and traffic lights by way of his underground movies about cars; and three poets from St. Mark's, one of whom had had the bad fortune to be wearing the same lime-green leather pants as Jesse Aarons. In all, an imposing assembly.

Joycelin's three best friends were also at hand, eager to see themselves as stars on the Europa's screen. There was Murray, a tall, lean, aging, gay Satanist with frizzed hair; his roommate, Eric, an office temporary, and Doris Del Ray (her stage name), who'd met Joycelin at a New School film history course in 1968. Doris now studied Jazz ballet with a teacher in Brooklyn Heights who had studied at Jacob's Pillow, long ago, with Ruth St. Denis. Consequently there was always a special sequence featuring Doris Del Ray, with choreography by Doris Del Ray, in each new installment of the work in progress. There she would be in her black tights, clawing at the air or convulsed into an expressive ball of pain or solemnly mounting and descending staircases swathed in remnants of sheer rayon, her long hair unbound, a priestess. This time it was a kind of temple scene, with Murray wearing his satanic vestments, on the steps of the Soldiers and Sailors Monument in Riverside Park. Murray also had a longish moment reading the Tarot. The camera studied each card intently while the soundtrack continued to play the temple theme, "Anitra's Dance." Eric's big moment came after the Tower was turned up. He picked up the card, scowled, and returned it to the deck. The music changed to "Ase's Death." He looked still grimmer: slow fade to black. As Eric's most salient character trait was an uninflected, sullen resentment that Murray regarded as butch, in *The Dance of Life* he symbolized Death and other negative vibrations. He never did much more than smoke and glower, but there was always a moment of him doing that somewhere in the middle of each reel, like Harpo's musical interludes in every Marx Brothers movie.

Contrary to the practice of Gary Webb, who scrupled, God-like, to efface the evidences of his own directing presence (even editing out footage into which his shadow might have strayed), Joycelin appeared abundantly in *The Dance of Life*—was, in fact, nearly coextensive with it. Here she was, at the start, striding down 8th Avenue toward the camera and into Donald's life. Now (with Donald still aiming the camera) she was fiddling with the dials on the phonograph (in tribute to the *Orpheus* of Cocteau). Holding up the record sleeve of *Revolver*. Feeding a squirrel in Central Park. Standing in the empty band shell and clapping her hands with enigmatic ill temper. (They'd had their first argument, and she was making fun of him.)

Here was Joycelin gluing acoustical egg cartons to the walls of her bedroom, and regluing them as they fell off. Here she was coming down 8th Avenue again. You could see the smile being jarred from her mouth as she walked. The expression that lingered in the closeup was one of mild, moist avidity. Someone in the theater (it sounded like Helen Emerson) actually snickered, but then it was time for Doris and Murray to do their thing on the temple steps, a sequence so typical of the foundation's offerings that no one dared say boo.

Joycelin next accepted a bouquet of pilfered tulips from Doris's hand, Doris having become a statue. Cut to Joycelin's favorite M. C. Escher poster, then pan down to Joycelin arranging the tulips in a glass. Then, in a moment of understated candor, the camera (with Joycelin guiding it now) examined Donald's clothing draped over a semideflated inflatable chair. Clouds scudded, Squirrel Nutkin nibbled away, the Hudson flowed softly by, and she ended her song with a reprise of herself advancing in slow motion down 8th Avenue, while, voice-over, she intoned a stanza from a poem she'd found in *Strengths*, a mimeo magazine of feminist poetry:

> *i love you*
> *for the way you see*
> *Innermost Me*
> *i love you*
> *for the strong caress*
> *of your fingers in my heart*
> *& how they always seem to know*
> *what parts are spoiled*

> *& pass them over*
> *to pull out treasures*
> *that I never knew were mine*
> *until you gave them to me*

The terminal closeup of Joycelin's face slowly faded to white. As the last wisps of eyebrow evanesced, a wee small voice went on:

> *i love you*
> *for the self-beauty*
> *i behold*
> *gleaming like diamonds*
> *in the priceless setting*
> *of your eye*

The applause stopped short of an ovation, and after that, in the discussion period, no one had anything to discuss. Ordinarily Donald could have got the ball rolling, but the poem, which had been added to the soundtrack as a last-minute valentine surprise, had thrown him off his usual moderating form.

He started the next movie, a slapstick parody of *Star Trek* by a ninth-grader at the Bronx High School of Science. People laughed at it perhaps more than it deserved. Joycelin got up in the middle and left the theater. After a short argument with Eric, Murray followed her out.

One forgets, during one's own romances, that it is a curse to fall in love. This time, for Donald, this had been apparent from the start, nor would it ever cease to be apparent. He was appalled at his heart's election. But there it was—he loved her. Worse, he lusted after her continually with the fixated, somnambulistic desire of Peter Lorre in *M* or a bride of Dracula. Waking he thought of her, sleeping he dreamed of her. It was the real thing, which there is no resisting.

After hours at the Europa, if he were not in demand at her apartment on East 13th, he would watch, entranced, reel after reel of *The Dance of Life* (which earlier had borne the title *Dance of the Moon-Girl*) and wonder: why? why me? why Mimi?

Mimi was his pet name for her (Squirrel Nutkin was hers for

him), after Puccini's Mimi, and in particular after the Mimi of Marguerite Ruffino, of the Ruffino Opera Company, which put on grand operas at an Off-Broadway theater on Monday nights, when it was closed. The company was financed by Marguerite's husband, a retired fireman, and in every production she sang the leading soprano role with a headlong, blissed-out inadequacy that kept her fans coming back steadily for more. Donald had seen her in *Aïda*, in *Norma*, in *Così fan tutte*, and in *La Gioconda*, but her greatest role, surely, was Mimi. No *Bohème* had ever been sadder, or truer to life, than the Ruffino's.

Pity—that had been Donald's downfall. All his life he had loved losers, losing, loss. At zoos his favorite animal was the yak, yearning hopelessly behind its bars for the peanuts no one wished or dared to feed it. He had pretended to find a higher wisdom in the more kindly varieties of ignorance, a Woolfean beauty in faces that were unarguably ill-formed and hidden forces throbbing in the filmic daydreams of the weak, the lazy, and the incompetent. Seeing this vice apotheosized in the love he felt for Joycelin did nothing to diminish his passion for her, but it did enable him to see how thoroughly he resented everyone else who took up space in his life. His friends! He wanted nothing but to be rid of them. No, even more he wanted a revenge for the decades he had spent praising their meretricious work—and he began to see how, beautifully and without a single overt betrayal, he might obtain it.

Unless she were filming and needed the light, Joycelin slept till two or three o'clock. This, together with the penchant of most twenty-year-olds for self-examination, allowed her, even after a second bout of love-making, to go on talking all night long—about her past, about her latest ideas for *The Dance of Life*, about what she'd do with his apartment if it were hers, about Murray and Doris and her boss at May's department store, where she worked four nights a week in accounts. Her boss had it in for her.

"Because," she explained one night, "I'm Jewish."

"I didn't know you were Jewish."

The burning tip of her cigarette bobbed up and down in the dark. "I am. On the side of my mother's grandmother. Her name was Kleinholz."

"But that doesn't necessarily mean—"

"People think Shrager is Jewish, but it isn't."

"It never occurred to me to think so. You don't *look* Jewish."

"People can sense it in me."

She was fired three days later. Proof, if any proof were needed, that anti-Semitism had struck again.

She was certain that Donald was concealing his true opinion of her. The books in his bookcase, the records on his closet shelves were unlike her books and records. Chance remarks required long footnotes of explanation. His friends were inattentive, and she didn't find their jokes funny. He said their humor was just a shorthand form of gossip, but that was no help. If they talked in riddles, how could she ever be sure it wasn't *her* they were gossiping about? Anyhow (she wanted him to know), her friends didn't care much for *him* either. Murray thought he was a phony. He'd done a chart of Donald and found out terrible things.

The easiest way to calm her at such times was not to urge the sincerity of his admiration, but to make love. She seemed to take his uxoriousness as her due, never offering any of those erotic concessions that a typical underdog believes will earn the ravished gratitude of the beloved, just lying back and yielding to his ardors. It astonished him, in his more reflective moments, how accepting she was of her own substandard goods. A Nigerian tribesman who has come into possession of a Land Rover could not have been more reverently admiring of his treasure than was Joycelin of the machineries of her flesh. Mirrors never fazed her, and she could pass by any shop window in the city and instantly translate its manikins into images of self. She wasn't (she knew) pretty, not in any conventional way at least, but the fairies who'd presided at her birth had made up for the lack with other gifts, and the light of them shone in her eyes. This was how her father had explained the matter to her in the once-upon-a-time of Cleveland, and that mustard seed had grown into a perduring, mountain-moving faith.

And yet she was uneasy. She revealed that in high school she had been known as Miss Bug. Once she'd taken a beginners' class with Doris's teacher in Brooklyn Heights and realized that the woman was making fun of her behind her back.

"That's what hurts, you know. Because you have to pretend you haven't noticed. Why couldn't she just come out and criticize me in the open? I know I'm no Pavlova or anything, but still. With a little more encouragement I'd have got the hang of it. I'm a born dancer, really. Murray thinks I must have been a ballerina in one of my previous lives. There's certain pieces of music that when I hear them it's like *The Red Shoes* all over again."

"You shouldn't let one person's opinion get you down like that."

"You're right, I know. But still."

She waited. He knew what she wanted from him, and it aroused him to be able, expertly, to supply it. It was easy in the dark. "You know, Mimi, the simplest things you do, just walking across a room maybe, or sitting down to eat, they have a kind of strange gracefulness. It *is* like dancing."

"Really? I don't try to."

"It's probably unconscious. Like a cat."

"Yeah?"

She wanted more, but he didn't have any immediately at hand. All he could think of was Cupcake, his super's fat, spayed calico, who rode the elevator up and down all day in the hope of getting to the garbage in the basement.

"Penny for your thoughts," she insisted.

"I was thinking about us."

An egg carton fell from the wall.

She waited.

"I was thinking how sometimes it's as though there's been a disaster, like in *The Last Man on Earth*, if you ever saw that."

"*I* feel like that at times. Completely alone."

"Except in my scenario you're there too. Just you and me and the ruins."

"Why you dirty old man! You're the one who's like a cat—an old tomcat. Stop that!"

"I can't, baby. Anyhow, we've got to get the world repopulated again."

"No, seriously, Squirrel Nutkin. You've just given me an incredible idea for the next part of *Dance*. And if I don't write it down I might forget."

She was up till dawn. Scribble, scribble, scribble.

He would arrange get-togethers with his oldest, dearest, so-called friends and let the fact of Joycelin sink in as they ate her parsimonious stews and meatloaves. Then, when the dishes had been cleared away, they'd watch *The Dance of Life*. With a soldierlike pleasure in his own remorseless fidelity, he squeezed wan compliments from his boggled colleagues. There were years and years of debts to be collected in this way, and Donald was careful never to exact more than the interest on the principal, so that in a few months he might press for renewed courtesies.

With Joycelin, increase of appetite grew by what it fed on, and when the first faltering praises trickled to a stop—the strained comparisons to Merce Cunningham or tantric art—she would nod demurely (making a note of such novelties in her mental notebook) and then ask for *criticism*. She admitted she was young and had rough edges. While in one sense her faults were part of her Gestalts (and therefore sacrosanct), on the other hand she was still growing and learning, and so any advice was welcome. For instance, in the long tracking shot of Doris, did the degree of jiggle perhaps exceed the ideal? Did the uncertainty of what was happening detract from the vision she'd meant to get across? Most guests survived these minefields by adopting the theory offered them—that all their hostess needed was a little more know-how vis-à-vis equipment, a little polish to bring out the natural beauty of the grain.

However. There were, inevitably, a handful who lacked the everyday aplomb to conceal their honest horror. Of these Mike Georgiadis was the most shameless, as well as the most cowardly, for he didn't even wait for the bedsheets to be tacked up screenwise on the wall before he was in flight, leaving poor Helen Emerson and Rafe Kramer to cope on their own. Helen in her day had soaked up god only knew how many fifths of Donald's Jim Beam, and Rafe had been dumping his little abnormalities into Donald's all-accommodating psychic lap for half their lifetimes, like an eternal festival of the murky, lubricious movies for which he had once won, with the wind of Donald's reviews in his sails, a Ford Foundation grant, no less. Even *they* betrayed him that night. Helen first, by bursting out, at the end of the jug of Gallo hearty burgundy, with the awful pronouncement that Joycelin's case was hopeless. That she was not an artist. That she never could be an artist, and that surely in her heart of hearts she must know this too.

In the face of such gorgon truths, what use was there talking about camera angles, shooting ratios, film stocks? Joycelin became tearful and appealed to Rafe.

Rafe was mute.

Helen, with implacable good will, said was it so important after all? People fussed too much about art. There were other things. Life. People. Pleasure. Love. Enlightenment.

Joycelin turned to stone.

Donald bit the bullet. "Helen," he said, echoing her tone of creamy reasonableness, "you *know* that what you're saying just isn't so. When you consider the budgets that Joycelin has had to work with, I think she's made better films than any of us. They're utterly honest. They're like doorways straight into her heart."

"Better than any of us?" Rafe insisted with mild amaze.

"Damned right."

"We're the has-beens," Helen declaimed, slipping into her English accent. "The bankrupts. The burnt-out cases. Isn't that so, Donald?"

"*I* didn't say it."

"And Gary?" Rafe demanded. "Is he another has-been?"

"You know how much I've always admired Gary's work, Rafe. But yes, I do think *The Dance of Life* is right up there with the best things Gary Webb has ever done. And Joycelin's still growing."

It was enough. Joycelin's composure was restored, and she it was who smoothed these waters with the assurance that nothing was worth old friends losing their tempers over. The Sara Lee cheesecake must be thawed by now. Why didn't they eat it?

The September issue of *Footage* had a long essay by Donald about *The Dance of Life*. He waited till it was in print to show Joycelin. As she read the article, a look came into her eyes. A look such as you might glimpse on a baby's wholly contented face, when its every need has been fulfilled: the understanding, for the first time, that there is a Future and that it will suffice.

Afterward he regretted that he hadn't thought to film her at that moment, for he was beginning to think of *The Dance of Life* as his own movie too, and even, in an odd way, to believe in it.

Donald had three rooms in a brownstone around the corner from the Europa. Since he'd been there time out of mind, his rent was less than Joycelin's, though she had only a narrow studio with a bathroom that she had to share with Murray. Donald's apartment, though no less ratty in its essentials, was of a less effortful kind of grunginess than hers. The furniture was off the streets or inherited from friends. Never had he deceived himself into attempting improvements, not by so much as a pine bookshelf. Things piled up of their own accord, on window sills and table-tops, in corners and closets, and increasingly they were Joycelin's things: her stereo (after it had been repaired); her paperbacks; her seven coleus plants; the Escher poster, a rug, a chair; most of her clothes, even the precious Bolex Rex-4 and the rest of her equipment, since his neighborhood was marginally safer and the windows had bars.

At last, after a serious talk, they agreed they were being ridiculous in keeping up two apartments. Even if it meant forfeiting her two months' deposit, wasn't that better than paying rent forever for a place that they spent so little time in and that had never been more anyhow than a temporary expedient?

So they borrowed Lloyd Watts's station wagon, and early one Tuesday morning they loaded it with whatever was still worth salvaging from East 13th Street, which was not a lot. Most painful to relinquish was an armchair that Joycelin had schlepped all the way from Avenue A, but she had to admit it was too bulky and probably (serviceable as it still was) full of roaches. There was a problem too with the toaster and the electric coffeepot, since Donald already had the best Korvette's could offer. But you can't just leave armchairs and appliances behind, like the old bags and paint cans under the sink. So, even though he didn't answer his door, it was determined that Murray was to be the inheritor of these and other orphaned articles: a lidless blue roasting pan, some empty flowerpots, a can of turtle food for the turtles that had died, a wealth of coat hangers, and a bicycle pump. Joycelin didn't have a key to Murray's room, but she knew how to jimmy his lock.

The room was painted a uniform, satanic black—floor, walls, ceiling, window—and all the light bulbs were gone from the sockets. They might very well have moved in all the presents without seeing Murray at all if Donald hadn't thought to light the room by opening the refrigerator door.

Their first thought was burglars. But burglars would not have dressed Murray so carefully in his cabalistic coat and hat and left him in the middle of a pentagram. No, it was Nembutals, as it had been twice before.

The reasons were not far to seek. Only a week after meeting Jesse Aarons at that fateful Sunday screening of *The Dance of Life*, Eric had got a part in a gay porn feature called *The Boys in the Bathroom*, and now he was living in a sado-masochistic commune in Westbeth. He wouldn't even talk to Murray on the phone. At the same time, more delicately but no less definitely, Joycelin had left Murray in order to mount the ladder of *her* success. He couldn't even be her cameraman now because of Donald. What was left?

They got him to Bellevue in the station wagon, and his stomach was pumped out in time. All the way back to 13th Street, where they'd forgotten to close the doors, Joycelin couldn't get over her awesome intuition. What force had led her to Murray at his darkest hour and made her break down his door?

Then she remembered the Tower. Right there in *The Dance of Life* was the answer, plain as day. From the moment he'd turned up that card, she should have known. Perhaps (was it so impossible?) she had!

Next day she was back at Bellevue with Murray's billfold (he needed his Medicaid I.D.), a pillowcase full of fresh underwear and socks, and the old Bolex Rex-4 around her neck. The guard wouldn't let her into the elevator with her camera (these were the days of the Willowbrook scandal, and warnings were out), and so the only footage she could get to illustrate this momentous chapter of her life was some very dark shots of the lobby and her argument with the nurse, and a long, careful pan of hundreds and hundreds of windows, behind one of which, unseen by Joycelin and never to be seen by her again, a pacified Murray in clean blue pajamas was playing dominoes with a Jehovah's Witness, who had threatened to jump from the balcony of Carnegie Hall during a Judy Collins concert until an usher convinced him not to.

At Christmas, Donald spent a small fortune on Joycelin, his jo. In addition to such basic too-muchness as perfume, an amber necklace, and a Ritz Thrift Shop mink, there was: a cased set of Japanese lenses and filters, a four-hundred-foot magazine for the

Bolex with sixteen giant spools of Kodak Four-X, a professional tripod with a fluid pan head, three quartz lighting heads in their own carrying case, a Nagra quarter-inch tape recorder, assorted mikes, and a mixer. He'd stopped short of an editing machine, reflecting that there'd be time for that extravagance later.

When all these treasures had been neatly wrapped in the most expensive gold paper with bushy red satin bows and stowed beneath and about the Christmas tree, itself a monument to his fiscal incontinence, he felt, supremely, the delirium of his own self-inflicted loving-madness. O *sink hernieder!* And he was sinking. At last he could understand those millionaires in Balzac who squander their fortunes on floozies, or those doctors and lawyers in Scarsdale and White Plains whose savage delight it is to see their money transmogrified into tall gravestones of coiled hair surmounting their wives' irredeemable faces, into parabolas of pearls declining into the dry crevasses between two withered dugs, into the droll artifice of evening gowns, whose deceits, like the sermons of Episcopalians, no one is expected to believe.

The unwrapping began as a responsible masque of gratitude and surprise and ended in genuine anxiety infused with disbelief. Without working out the arithmetic, she could not but wonder how, unless he were a stockbroker in disguise, Donald could have afforded all of this.

At last, when they were sitting down with their eggnogs in front of the electric yule log, she had to ask.

"It's simple. I sold the magazine."

"You sold *Footage*. That's terrible!"

"I'm keeping my column in it. That's down in writing. All I'm giving up is the drudgery, and Jesse is welcome to that."

"Jesse Aarons?" she asked, as he snuffled in the loose flesh of her neck.

"You see. . . . " He curbed the stallion of desire, leaned back in the nest of handcrafted pillows that had been Joycelin's merry gift to him, and exposited. "Jesse had the idea, some while ago, that there should be a *serious* magazine about skin-flicks. Something that would do for porn what *Cahiers* did for Hollywood, make it look intellectual. At the time I'd used a couple of his articles along those lines, but I couldn't see taking the whole magazine in that direction."

"I should hope not. But then why—"

"Five thousand dollars."

Joycelin set down her eggnog on the new Nagra and became serious. "But just last week, Donald, Jesse *borrowed* eighty dollars from you."

"The money doesn't come directly from Jesse. Harold Bachofen was the purchaser, but his name won't go on the masthead. Though Arnold's will, of course. Harold screwed Jesse out of the profits on *Ear, Nose, and Throat* last year, and he's giving him *Footage* by way of an apology. I think he wants a slice of his next feature now that Jesse's star is on the rise."

"I still don't think you should have done it. I mean, *Footage* was worth a lot more than five thousand dollars. It's the most respected magazine in the field."

"Every issue of that respected magazine puts me two hundred dollars in the red. When I'm lucky. We've got better things to do with our money."

"You should at least have waited to find out whether I get my CAPS grant or not. If Helen Emerson can get a CAPS grant, I don't see why I can't."

"Absolutely, Mimi my love. All in good time. But meanwhile, five thousand dollars is five thousand dollars." He poured the last of the eggnog into her glass.

She sipped and thought. Fake firelight from the yule log rippled over her Art Deco negligee. She struck an attitude—elbow propped on the arm of the couch, chin resting on the back of her hand—suggestive of close attention to music not audible to other ears than hers. At such moments Donald was sure she was thinking: "Is he looking at me now?" But this time her thoughts had truly been on a larger, philosophic scale, for when she came out of it, it was to declare, with all the hushed solemnity of a presidential press secretary, that Donald had done the right thing and that she was proud of him. And very happy.

The first issue of *Footage* to come out under Jesse Aarons's aegis had for its cover a still from *The Dance of Life* that showed Eric in a denim jacket, squinting at the smoke of his cigarette. It looked every bit like a face on the cover of a real magazine. Joycelin gazed and gazed, insatiable. There was also another nice little mention in Donald's column.

"I wonder. . . . "

"What do you wonder, my love?"

"Whether I shouldn't try and get in touch with Eric again. I mean, he has been so much a part of *Dance* right from the start. Just because he isn't with Murray anymore—"

"What about Murray? Did you ever find out his address?"

"No, and I don't care if I ever do. The bastard."

Murray had gone off to San Francisco without ever saying good-bye, much less thanking her for his life. The transition between concern for Murray's mental health to bitterness at this snub had been difficult to accomplish.

"Bastard?"

"Well, I wasn't going to tell you this, but you know how Murray was always telling everyone how he was a Scorpio? He's not. When I had to bring him his things to the hospital, I looked in his billfold. Where it says date of birth on his draft card, the date was January 28, 1937. An Aquarius! His *moon* isn't even in Scorpio for god's sake. I looked it up, and it's in Capricorn."

"He probably thought he'd be more interesting as a Scorpio."

"Of course that's what he thought. But that doesn't make it right, does it? There's one thing I can't stand, and that's a liar. I mean, if your own friends *lie* to you, how can you believe *anything*?"

The wedding was in June, at St. Mark's in the Bowery. Joycelin's parents were to have come, but at the last moment (not unexpectedly) her mother came down with shingles, so Harold Bachofen acted *in loco parentis* and did very well. Joycelin's gown was a collaboration between herself and Doris Del Ray—a white silk muumuu swathed in tulle, with a veil and train that were one and the same. Donald dressed white tie, as did Harold Bachofen. Everyone else came in whatever they regarded as regal, which included, in at least one instance, drag.

The theme of the wedding, in any case, was not to have been fashion, but *film*. Everyone who owned or could borrow a camera was told to bring it to St. Mark's and shoot, the resulting trousseau of footage to be incorporated into a single grandiose wedding march in *The Dance of Life*. Since the invitation list included everyone in underground film who hadn't actively snubbed Joycelin, the results were gratifyingly spectacular. Donald stopped counting cameras at twenty-three. As a final dollop of authentication, a news team from *Eyewitness News* appeared just as the bride was being led to the altar. (Donald's former brother-in-law, Ned Miles, was now an executive at Channel Seven.) The wedding, alas, was squeezed out of the news that night by an especially sinister double murder in Queens, but the news team made it into *The Dance of Life*. They were the only people in the whole church who seemed at all astonished at what was happening.

And Joycelin? She was radiant. True movie stars, Donald had theorized once in *Footage*, actually receive energy from the camera, or from the cameraman, like plants getting energy from the sun. They become more alive, more definite, more completely who they are, like the dead on the Day of Judgment when they arise, wartless and cleansed of all the local accidents of character: the skeletons of their essential selves. So too Joycelin, whose special and enthralling awfulness always awoke to greatest vividness when she was being filmed. And today . . . today, with cameras springing up like daisies in a field, today there was no reckoning her transcendency. Roland Barthes said of Garbo that her face represented a kind of absolute state of the flesh, which could be neither reached nor renounced, a state in which "the flesh gives rise to mystical feelings of perdition." In this respect Joycelin and Garbo were much alike.

The filming continued at The Old Reliable, where the reception was held. As Donald had been temporarily overwhelmed, Joycelin and Doris took it on themselves to collect the contributions to the Foundation for Free Cinema, which was what they'd requested in lieu of conventional wedding gifts. People got drunk too quickly, a crush developed, and Jesse Aarons got into a fight. The bride and groom left early.

Joycelin was kittenish, not to say petulant, in the cab, and when they arrived home she insisted on a bride's prerogative of having the bedroom to herself. Donald undressed down to his shorts, and then passed the time drinking from the bottle of Asti Spumante he'd rescued from the reception. It was flat. He didn't feel so wonderful himself. Great and long-awaited events do take it out of you.

He tried to get into the bedroom but Joycelin had locked the door, so he watched *Eyewitness News*. They showed the actual bloodstains in the stairwell where the woman had been stabbed. Forty-seven times. And the woman's niece as well.

At last she said to come in.

The dear old Bolex, on its new tripod, with its four-hundred-foot magazine in place, was set up facing the bed. The quartz lighting heads blazed down on the turned-back sheets like the desert sun.

"Surprise!" She was wearing nothing but the one-piece veil and train.

He could not pretend to disapprove on either moral or esthetic grounds. Joycelin had not only seen *Reel 168*—she'd read Donald's reviews of it. The principle was the same. But still.

"Mimi, darling. . . . I don't think I can. Not at this moment."

"That's all right, Donald. Take your time."

He went and sat at the foot of the bed, facing the eye of the lens. "Any other time, but not tonight. That reception got me down, I think. Seeing all those people I haven't seen in so long."

"You don't have to apologize to *me*. Just sit right where you are and say what you're feeling. Whatever it may be. Now that we're married it's like we're just one person. *Dance* is yours now as much as it's mine. Really."

She started the camera rolling. Unconsciously he'd placed his hands in front of his listless crotch. He could not look up.

She held out the directional mike. "Just say anything. Whatever you're thinking. Because whatever *is*—is right."

He was thinking about failure, which seemed, tonight, the universal fact of human life. But he couldn't say that. His thoughts were sealed inside his head like the documents in the cornerstone of a building. They could never come out.

"Hey there! Squirrel Nutkin! Look at the camera, huh? Say cheese."

He looked up at the camera and began to cry. For her, for him, for all his friends—for the dance of life.

The Joycelin Shrager Poems

*Reading good poetry will make anyone feel better. But it can
also help you if you are emotionally disturbed.*
    —Dr. Smiley Blanton, *The Healing Power of Poetry*

Intro

Hi and hello from Andy Lowe, here to introduce a mitey-fine new
poet by the name of Joycelin Shrager, whom a few of you may
already know as the guiding lite at moonchild press & who was
a leading underground filmmaker before that.

   Joycelin is an original.

   There's lots of poets who'd like to be originals, myself included,
but to Joycelin it just comes naturally. She sings in a voice all her
own. There is nothing else quite like it & I guess the reason it's
me writing this intro & not Bill or Larry or Bernadette is because
it was in my Wednesday nite poetry workshop at St. Mark's that
Joycelin discovered that unique voice of hers which is so disturb-
ing, so weird & so funny!

   Here's the story.

   The workshop had been running for a couple weeks already
when Joycelin showed up one night in November, looking a few
sizes larger than life in a Mexican blanket doing time as a poncho.
Even blanketless, Joycelin is pretty large, having decided, now that
she's no longer a filmmaker, that dieting sucks. At that time I was
new to the St. Mark's scene, having connected with it when I was
teaching awareness at Naropa in Boulder, & so I hadn't seen any
of the films Joycelin was known for. To me she was just another
depressive overweight teenager & the sheaf of poems she read
aloud that nite confirmed my first impression. Sloppy sentimental

bilge jingling with lovey-dovey rimes, like some Victorian Rod McKuen. I did what I always do when a kid hands in that kind of crap—I ripped the whole bundle to shreds. Then, while Joycelin, who is really pretty much in touch with her feelings, sat there crying puppydog tears, I explained, using her deconstructed poems, how to make hash-browns with the recipe developed by old Bull Burroughs. After a few shuffles and splices, some of Joycelin's lines didn't look half-bad, & she seemed to perk up after I'd shown how much *potential* energy there was in her language, once it had been liberated from its context.

Well, the next week Joycelin shows up with a whole sheaf of her own hash-browns & some of them were genuinely strange. Maybe it was the sense of splicing she developed as a filmmaker, but whatever the reason some of her line-breaks had the snap of a broken limb. Gerard Malanga, look out, you've got competition!

That was a good beginning, but getting Joycelin to write in a non-aleatory way from the center of her spiritual energies was not an overnite job. The one major feeling she was directly in touch with turned out to be self-pity, and self-pity is a tricky theme for anyone but a really disciplined poet like Plath or Lifshin. Beginners do best to stick to affirmation, then move on to anger for like the second semester & save the pain for when they're really sure of themselves.

Anyhow, putting aside those reservations, I was determined to help Joycelin become the best poet she could, since it is my basic conviction about teaching poetry that *absolutely anyone can become a publishable poet*. All it takes is a few nudges in the right direction. Of course, this idea is not original with me. Kenneth Koch was the one who put it to the test by taking a class of fourth or fifth graders and turning the lot of them into Little-League Robert Lowells. Then, to top that, he went & did the same thing with the vegetables in an old folks home. Well, if Koch could get those kind of results from that lot, then there had to be some way for me to get Joycelin writing from her chakras.

Joycelin made a lot of progress that year in various directions, mostly in technical things like learning *not* to rime, which was difficult for her. Then on the nite of April 1, 1978, came her big breakthru. That was the class when I suggested that everyone write his or her Nobel Prize Acceptance Speech, which was also going to be the theme of the next issue of my mag *Dial-Tone*. A whole underground galaxy of New York School notables had agreed to respond to that What-if, for it truly is a fantasy that any writer can get off on. Talk about Wishes, Dreams & Lies!

Just suppose, I told the class, that you're 50 years old & looking back on your creative lifetime, instead of 20 or 25 & still looking ahead. Just explain what you're feeling from the perspective of the person you'd like to become. That was the assignment & somehow it touched Joycelin's basic creative button like nothing else so far. Suddenly she stopped experimenting & wrote with everything she had—hands, feet, heart & soul. The result is the first poem in this book, "i am just a plain poet." Joycelin had found her voice poetically & there was nothing now that was ever going to make that voice shut up.

Already the wish/dream/lie of that first "pome" has begun to come true. Joycelin's poems have appeared in a dozen little mags, from my own *Dial-Tone* to the *American Poetry Review*! She has won her second CAPS grant (her first was for filmmaking) and given readings all over the place including the Y! She was interviewed by *13th Moon*, and invited to become a member of PEN!

People who knew Joycelin back before she'd started publishing poems that made her famous say that they're surprised at her success. But not me. Rite from the nite of that April 1st class I could see that Joycelin had the one great essential for poetic success. She had a faith in herself that nothing could challenge, & because she did, we can too.

—Andy Lowe
Sept. 1, 1983
Boulder, Colorado

Contents

i am just a plain poet

i am just a plain poet
the way pete seeger
is just a plain singer

no frills about what i do
you don't need big-deal critics
to tell you what my pomes mean

i know i'm not as good a
poet as many others
who aren't as famous as me
but that's because they can't
speak to the audience i can

speak to the audience of people
who may not be very bright
or in the top third of their class
but who still want to be good

to be understood and appreciated

those are my people
you can't expect them to like
a subtle poet like john ashbery
(who i have to confess doesn't make
a scrap of sense to me)

not everyone is going to dig
even anne waldman who is my own
personal candidate for the greatest

modern american poet (my friend
rod mckuen agrees) anne is so
damn life-affirming which is great
if you've got the sort of life
you want to affirm
                              a lot of us
don't we've got to work at lousy jobs
we're stuck in ratty apartments
we tend to be unpopular
except with each other

as i say these are my people
& my press Moonchild Press
communicates with them directly
on their own level because i
am one of them a moonchild
moonsister flesh of their
flesh mind of their mind

they aren't all simple people
by any means they aren't all good
they only want to be good
but they do think about things
like the meaning of life
they can recognize the loveliness
of stars & flowers & animals in zoos
& the terrible sorrow too

some of them have learned to love
deeply
              tenderly
                          & true

the smart people have always listened
to my people's songs but they've never
heard their poetry

                              until me
until Joycelin Shrager!

something people don't realize

something people don't realize
is how tragic it is to be fat
believe me it's no joke though
you'd never know that from the way
people act / i suffer from overweight
& of course i'd like to look like
faye dunaway or leslie caron
but even at my most thin
seven years ago i was no
miss america/ my mother's
the same as me loves to eat
can't keep away from the icebox
can't stop snacking becomes deeply
depressed on the second day of a diet
she's learned the only way to be even a
little happy is to give in to cravings
right away/ they say fat people have
more of a sense of humor than the
rest of you/ i guess they don't
know about our tears i guess
they haven't seen us look
ashamed going into the
special departments
set apart for fatties
i guess when you're
thin it doesn't
matter much
what fat people
must suffer

i who have gone through the whole gamut

i who have gone through the whole gamut
of experience the heights of artistic
success & the depths of grief loss
& humiliation have this to say to you
the way to be happy is to live totally
in the present moment to give yourself
up to the buttercups of spring
& the beautiful green lawns of a summer
afternoon when you've sneaked into a
cemetery to surrender yourself completely
to a doubledip icecream cone to relax
in a warm tub & float along
with rimsky-korsakov's scheherazade
or look into a baby's eyes & think
he's mine i made him inside
my own body i brought him to birth
with my own pain   for even pain
can be creative even the death
of a dearly loved spouse can be a source
of joy when you look out the window
& realize that everything in the universe
is mysteriously connected to everything
else including our dear ones gone to rest
including you donald tho i may never
understand why you left me suicide
is always so foolish but never mind
i'll always love you anyhow

minor poets are human too

minor poets are human too
& when we go out in the woods
& marvel at mushrooms & lie in the
sand & flip out for a great symphony
what we're feeling then is as
important to us as whatever
it was that wallace stevens felt when he
wrote all those poems that no one under
stands

      but what's even harder to under
stand about wallace stevens is how he
could be an insurance salesman
all those years he was a poet
at the same time   you'd think
he'd be too tired when he got home
from a day of canvassing

             my father tried
to sell insurance for a while after the
bankruptcy & didn't get anywhere
except he did sell a big policy to poor
donald which led to my founding
Moonchild Press in 1976

it was the same insurance company
that wallace stevens worked for way
back when   everything connects
mysteriously to everything else
in the world of the spirit

today i was almost put in jail

today i was almost put in jail
can you believe it   & all
because i went to my friend barbara
taplinger's dance recital in union square
part of the big SWEET 14 campaign
to get the pushers out of the park
which is maybe not such a bad idea
even if you enjoy the occasional joint
since most ordinary people buy their dope
at home from their friends   barbara
thinks differently she says
people who have to buy dope
on the street are the ones who probably
need it most of all & so they shouldn't
be discriminated against unfairly
she didn't mind her recital being part
of the SWEET 14 festival however
because she thot all the blacks & hispanics
would groove with it seeing as they like to
dance themselves   so anyhow the show started
with a very modernistic warming up
exercise to an old buddy holly record
a lot like some of twyla tharp's
things if you've ever seen those
it was guaranteed according to barbara
to grab their immediate attention
it certainly did everyone in the park
started crowding up behind the bunch of us
standing just in front of the stage
which was actually more what you would call

a platform after the buddy holly piece
barbara started dancing in earnest
accompanied by irving steiner on the moog
synthesizer irving is a very high-strung
musician who isn't used to playing
in an unstructured environment like union
square naturally he got flustered
& did one repeat too many which
barbara was unable to cope with since
she could not go on spinning one minute
longer they started over from the
beginning & that was when i heard
the first radio you know those giant
radios they call boxes one of those
it belonged to a kid sitting
way at the other end of the area we were
in but you could hear it over the moog
since the Prelude begins so quietly
"like a feather falling" irving wrote on the
score   fortunately irving had pulled himself
together & reacted like an old trooper
playing his moog louder than the radio
that's when someone right there
in the crowd turned on his radio
& then suddenly there were
a dozen radios all tuned to wktu disco 92
you couldn't hear anything else
barbara stopped dancing & just stood there
terrified & put-out whereas i simply felt
incredibly angry as tho everything i believed
in had been violated so without even
thinking about it i boosted myself up
onto the stage & said please please
lifting my arms up to get their attention
turn off your radios this isn't fair
to those of us who came to see the dance
i don't think they understood me
or maybe they couldn't hear anyhow one of them
jumped onto the stage beside me & started

dancing to the song on the radios
& there was me in the middle of it
angry as a coot shouting at all
the people who'd started dancing
all around the stage & then all over it
meanwhile irving & barbara had gone off to get
the police but in the wrong direction
because the police were already there
& i was the second person they arrested
they wouldn't listen to anything i said
& there was no sign of irving or barbara
finally at the precinct house i was allowed
to phone for a lawyer thank heaven
i remembered the name of the lawyer
we talked to during the rent strike
if it hadn't been for larry mccarthy
i might be in jail at this moment
another serious miscarriage of justice
when i told the story to edna
she seemed to think it was a scream
but it wasn't the least bit funny
if you were there & it was happening
to you poor barbara had to cancel
her big presentation next wednesday
in battery park because of the attention
the incident attracted on the Evening News
where all the blacks who got arrested
said they thot they were supposed
to get up & start dancing as a part
of the idea behind the concert
barbara in her interview said possibly
that was not a bad idea altho not
the one she had had in mind as a result
of saying which she may lose her caps grant
according to edna who gets inside
information at the very least
her grant won't be renewed
& you can't tell me blacks aren't to blame

hey everyone look at what's here

hey everyone look at what's here
look at this wonderful world of ours
with all those trees & the beautiful
flowers   can you understand why
they come in such complicated shapes
impossible to draw them or why light
bulbs work it's all part of the whole
amazing system which i don't think
anyone understands for once the professors
are in the same boat with the rest of us

which reminds me of an incredible fact
lewis carroll who wrote alice in wonder
land actually knew the alice in his
book and was sort of in love with her
he was a professor i think of mathematics
& he often took little alice out
in his boat   do you think she knew

if it had been i i wonder could i
have returned his wonderland love
the original alice didn't
but of course she had no way of knowing
that he was more than just another prof

bowling has been the great spirit

bowling has been the great spirit
ual experience of my life
i never thot i'd be able to do
anything physical until my friends
bonnie and donna took me to the bowling
alley just four blocks from where i live
& taught me to bowl
how to run up real fast
to the foul line & let rip
without thinking of where
the ball would go exactly
but just imagining the SMASH!
it'll make when it hits
zen bowling donna calls it
& it works at least for people
like me who rely on intuition
i'm bowling over 100 now
almost every game & tho
that may not seem like a lot
to most bowlers to me
it's pure glory

when i am sick science fiction

when i am sick science fiction
is my passion the more escapist
the better   none of that new
wave stuff   (that's for when i'm well &
prepared to meet challenges)

but conan & elric & tolkien
& anne mccaffrey those are my deities
i journey with them into the 4th
dimension of my head where i caress
the silken tresses of my steed & hear
the twanging of a magic harp

                        so imagine
how delighted i was this year
when my favorite sf author

              Silverbob

(that's robert silverberg in case
you didn't know) produced his first
novel in far too long combining
the jewellike mind-boggling intellectual
excitement of his New Wave achievements
with that old-fashioned Sense of Wonder
fans can go for   it's called

          lord valentine's castle

(any connection silverbob with
lord weary's castle by robert lowell
have i given away any secrets you sly fox)

well what can i say it was wonderful
his best book ever & it sold to paperback
for a lot of money too i'm told

so please silverbob please please
please keep writing don't
take another long vacation
like the last one when you thot
fandom hadn't been grateful we are
& to prove it i'm going to come
to the next worldcon & totally
smother you with appreciation
& silverbob remember
if you ever turn to poetry—
think of Moonchild Press

excuse the language

excuse the language
but i got so pissed off today
i just came to pieces
(can you believe i'm 34 years old
& still have to look in the
dictionary for the spelling of pieces)
now i can't even remember
what it was got me so angry
in the first place
no i do remember it's because
tomorrow i have to go on strike
all those years of being exploited
in offices without windows or
coffee breaks & being told i can't
wear a pants suit & not to smoke
& now when i've finally got a job
i like i have to go on strike

i suppose my fellow union members
are right we probably aren't paid
what we're worth but i'm just so pleased
to be paid anything to be creative
usually the only chance i have to be
creative is here on my smith-corona

what i do is paint pictures
not the kind you see in soho
galleries that cost thousands of
dollars but the cheapest kind
you can buy that are still genuine

oil paintings i specialize in
pictures of puppies & kittens
with big lovable warm brown eyes
also children dressed up as grownups
& sometimes ballerinas tho i haven't
completely got the hang of anatomy
especially fingers and knees

i am slower than the last person
who had my job maybe partly because
i'm new but also because i believe
in what i do i've been drawing
puppies & kittens so long as i can
remember: sincerity always makes
the big difference but especially for
creative people my paintings get sold
the minute they go into the shop
on 6th avenue whereas
some of the others which are technically
far superior to mine don't sell at all
or take a very long time
& i think the reason is sincerity

personally i think it's ridiculous
for artists to be in a union
if artists aren't individuals who is
but there's nothing i
as a single powerless person can do
so tomorrow i'll just have to carry
my sign in the picket line
like everybody else & hope
we reach an agreement with management soon

my assignment this week is a sonnet

for john godfrey

my assignment this week is a sonnet
fortunately it doesn't have to rime
as long is it has exactly 14 lines
it'll be ok my teacher andy lowe
who edits dial-tone in addition to
teaching says he honestly wants to
vomit when he sees rimes in a modern
poet tho there is no one who respects
the great traditions of english poetry
more than andy   take yr daily life
andy says & put it under the microscope
of poetry write a kind of newsletter
about yr inner secrets & yr friends
& if you've got more to say than
there's room for in 14 lines or not
enough don't worry the basic unit of
modern poetry is the human breath divine

gotta get my act together

for bernadette mayer

gotta get my act together
tuesday today & wednesday tomorrow
& no sox left in the drawer
no tab in the icebox
no windex no eggs no shampoo
no bread & my credit card has been
disqualified   but plenty of sunlight
in the morning & the moon at night
so everything's basically alright
in fact my life is finally so full
i really can't complain
i'm invited to richard kostalanetz's big
reading 2 weeks from now in a soho loft
& 2 days after that bernadette mayer
will read at st. mark's how about that
& this morning i got a really friendly
rejection from the Editor
of dial-tone handwritten no less
he said he liked my poem about
poor little rudolpho
which i wrote over 5 years ago
on the day rudolpho died
& about the way i cried
if there is a heaven for hamsters
i hope you're in it rudolpho
i don't care if that sounds sentimental
no more poetry for now
i have just got to get the laundry done
my life's such an amazing mess & i love it

if you know what i mean

for john ashbery
with love from joycelin

the way andy lowe explained it
is imagine there's a second you
in the same room with the first
you & talking into a phone
while you are talking into
another   now even tho neither
of you is actually listening
to what the other you is
saying you can't help over
hearing parts of it & picking
up on some of the ideas or at
the very least certain key
words & phrases basically that's
all ashbery is doing in as we
know so now andy told us
(this was all happening at st.
mark's where andy gives a work
shop every wednesday nite)
go thou & do likewise

the trouble is i can't really
believe i'm somebody i'm not
just cuz i'm writing on the other
side of the page it seems to me
i'm the same person i always was
(my eternal joycelin donald used
     to
say) only maybe a few minutes
     older
when i raised the problem to andy
he sd can't you pretend   okay
i'll pretend i'm in the other room
(not this one cuz i could see
myself if i were here) & i can
hear myself in there talking about
as we know by john ashbery
which even with andy's
     explanations
doesn't make much sense to me
     well
at least i'm willing to admit my
limitations which according to
andy is the source of real poetry
anyhow

i also raised the point of
how exactly do you know when to
switch sides   there's no rule he
     sd

what i mean sd donna is
     philosophy
goddammit what's ashbery if not
a philosopher & we're here talking

just rite on one side of the
page for a little while then switch
the thing to bear in mind is break
thru the constrictions of linear
thinking the brain after all has
two hemispheres   then knowitall
donna zerby sd we were being
wierdly superficial or is it
weirdly (never never change
a word never edit never revise
that's one of the workshop's
most basic rules) what do
you mean andy asked her using
his patented combination of
    mental
tai chi & the socratic method

about empty external forms
how about an example sd andy
well donna looked around in the
    book
for a while & then read some lines
which i would quote here except
for the problem of copyrite
& we all tried to figure out
what the philosophy was behind
    them
donna sd it was a philosophy of
    love
& andy sd it was about man's place
in relation to nature & i piped up
& sd maybe you're both saying
the same thing which pleased
    andy
& seemed to piss donna off
donna being such an arguer

you know sd andy maybe she's
    right
maybe we are saying the same
    thing
& what's more maybe the two
    voices
in ashbery's pome are both
saying the same thing too

no no no sd donna you've got it
assbackwards ashbery's showing us
that there isn't such a thing
as a single voice even his own
is broken into pieces

right right sd andy nodding his
head but listen to the two pieces
& what are they saying

they're saying just this exactly
this is the modern condition

have you ever gone up to the roof

have you ever gone up to the roof
& looked at the millions of twinklers
in the sky

        have you ever thought how
enormous the universe must be
& what a little speck in it you are
yourself

        i do constantly but then
i realize the wonderful fact
that i am me with both my legs
and my hand reaching up to pluck
the brightest star that's there

my sad brown eyes are always searching
searching for love searching
for someone who will really care

o my beloved where are you
if i have to wait much longer
i may commit suicide

            i know it's wrong
to talk like that even in a poem
but i'm so lonely tonight
& no one i telephone is home

1 2 3 4

Close Your Eyes Now

Let the big cockroach crawl over your face.
It's night, you're tired, we won't talk about
Reality here where the paralyzed ballerina
Moans in her wheeled bed. I love you. Sleep
Speaks. Its finger blackens. The air,
Conscious that it is air, relinquishes
Its claims. The heart names names:
Judith, Andrew, Sharon, Jerry, James.

Neurons fire and once again, slowly, night
Dawns. A tired accountant counts
The doorways, numbers the crumbling facades,
Waits endlessly before the broken elevator's
Gleaming doors. We must go in. There's the fun
Of undressing, and then the smearing of black
Makeup over sore muscles. I feel
Your tongue enter mine. The iron wheel

That lifts the sandwiched logs squeals
Warnings. I refuse to believe anyone
In the company would steal my clothes:
Perhaps the robbery wasn't real. I take
Your hand, and from the darkness high above
The stage a woolen scarf unreels
Towards my patient wrists. I'm bound.
Another load of bodies settles to the ground

With a lurch and a bump. I am next
But I refuse to be lifted to such a height:
The knots are loose. Judith, too, is

Terrified. Ah, but taste the tears that glitter
In the eyes of those who were wound up
Into the sky. Their fear is the merest
Spoonful of salt. Ecstatically their fingers feel
Each others' faces. I envy their ordeal.

I love you and I do not care if I am
Killed. Tell me the rules. Prepare
My blood. Make the light as bright
As you possibly can, but don't leave me
Here in this washroom, attended
By a wizened psychotherapist. Why
Must I wait? Earphones are clamped
Over my ears. The room gets more cramped,

Shrinks to the size of a toilet. The walls
Are scrawled with graffiti high as I can climb:
Mutilated genitalia, names of bones.
Hidden blowers emit whiffs of roach spray,
Cigarette smoke. The earphones explain
That all this awfulness is real and true.
I refuse to believe. Too much is at stake:
I ask for a blindfold and awake.

Selected Quirks

*It is an open question whether the moral status of mankind
has undergone an improvement in our times.*
        —Dr. Richard von Krafft-Ebing

Case One had masturbated all his life.
Case Two asked favors from the gardener's boy.
Case Three was twenty-nine and had no wife.
Case Four was fond of whips and corduroy.

Case Five experienced profound distress
During his semi-annual pollutions.
Case Six had lost two servants and a mistress
By his passion for electrocutions.

A father's tainted blood depraved Case Seven.
Case Eight was roused by gloves, Case Nine by shoes.
Case Ten had incest twice with Case Eleven.
But worse than these was Twelve, who would not choose.

Poem from the Pen

Through iron bars of pain & tears
Across the dustbowl of the years
I strain to touch my Susie's hand
But she is in another land

I could of been a boxing pro
But drugs & liquor laid me low
My children think of me with shame
I only got myself to blame

I killed a man—They buried me—
For forty years I won't be free
Across grey walls the shadows creep
While I rot like a compost heap

They say you shouldn't bear a grudge
But if I could I'd kill my judge
And hang the jury who hung me
Oh how I long for liberty

The Mad Governess

Observe, my dears, that creature there
Who has those flowers in her hair
And such an air of seeming proud;
Yet *I* would say her clothes are loud,
And there are lines about her face
That make it rather commonplace.
One really has to feel some pity
For the lower orders of the city.
Why *has* this mob invaded Kew?
Not, I daresay, to pursue
The Muse of Botany. Their bouquet,
If I may say so, is Botany Bay.

Now there's a child I'd diagnose
As having not too many clothes,
And those she has are rather plain;
But don't display the least disdain,
For it is very wrong, you know,
To pride ourselves on pomp and show.
By "plain" I meant a compliment.
Oh, William, now your twig is bent,
And it will never be a tree.
We must go back and buy another,
Or we will hear it from your mother.

A bench, at last! but I forget—
I may not smoke a cigarette
Before these brats. Or speak aloud
The thoughts that hover like a cloud
About my beating, beaten heart.

I must be calm. I must not start
To rave. Children, look: a slave
Auction! I mean, a bridal pair.
If you, dear Guinevere, *behave,*
Some day that is what you will wear.
Now sit and let me catch my breath.
The two of you will be my death.

Psalms of a Tax Accountant

I

The day is the machine
                        whose task it is

To remind me by its clanking
                        ever to be alert

To the news that trickles
                        down from heaven;

As thus, on wakening, I pray
                        shortly to receive

My breakfast.   Behold—
                        there on the counter

It is: two eggs over lightly
                        with a side of french.

As I perforate the yolks
                        I think how He

Exerts dominion
                        over a million and a million

Destinies as indirect
                        as the chickens'

Who have yielded me these eggs
                    or the waitresses' who served them.

I rejoice as I pay my bill
                    at the marvel of inflation,

That indispensable crutch
                    to the tottering myth of progress.

Along the rows of friendly shops,
                    up in the mirrored cage

Of the elevator: as I go
                    I hum a hymn of

Private woe. The cypress
                    of my grief appears

Within the mirrors
                    like donkey ears.

II

My work is my prayer:
                    each anxious altercation

A song of praise to the One
                    whose Will obscure I read

In the accounts I help to hide
                    from the Mammon of taxes.

My Lord forever amazes me
                    by the aptness of his system

Of punishments and rewards.
                    I have seen the highest

Income brackets brought low;
                              I have witnessed the wise man

Thriving among green lawns.
                              Selah, my lips must form

Those phonemes and those awful vowels
                              by whose forbidden utterance

I shall ultimately enter the pastures
                              of an all-rewarding rest.

III

It is then, at the hour
                              of the aperitive,

That I allow myself one
                              Prelude of Debussy

By way of accompaniment
                              to a rote prayer of thanks.

Thanks, Lord, I pray,
                              for the fictions of today.

Bless my heart, and bless my house;
                              make me docile as a mouse

Rescued from savagery
                              and taught to serve

As entertainment for
                              some possible Messiah.

Such a child as now descends
                              from the springtime of his toys

Into my arms and through my blood,
                      whose deepest mystery

I've ceded him. Lord,
               what's for dinner?

The Bride of Baron Death

In a house, somewhere, with a tower
    And a single burning light
(The house is stone, the candle flickers),
    A table has been set

For two, the wines have been selected,
    And you call upstairs
(To me): "Dinner's ready, dearest
    Love—come down!"

Above the fireplace (the fireplace
    Is cold) a portrait hangs:
You, in your youth—another face
    Than that you wore tonight.

I wonder at the change. I hear your
    Footsteps on the stairs,
Your voice through the thickness of the door,
    Asking, softly, whether

My gown's been laid out on the bed. It is
    There. "A minute,"
I beg. "A minute more." Your smile
    Watches from the wall.

(The wind groans. Windows rattle.)
    I would pry off this ring,
But my knuckles have swollen with the cold,
    And my heart is hollow.

Fool's Mate

There is a game that plays a man,
They sell it as Romance™.
The user starts by having to choose:
(A) He's a loser; (B) He's a fan;
   (C) He teaches dance.

Since everybody opts for (C),
We enter a cruiser, the *Libertine Belle*,
That is re-equipped as a luxury ship
With sumptuous ballrooms on every deck
   And furnaces hot as hell.

There beneath the chandeliers
You offer instruction in Tango and Mambo,
   In Foxtrot, in Samba,
In the Waltz and all the latest rages—
   The Stripping of Gears,
The Shaking of Spears, the Rock of Ages.

Then one evening the Maître d'
Brings a note to your table,
   Which reads, "*Mein Herr*,
Or *Gnädige Frau* (as the case may be),
Leave this ship if you are able.
   If not, beware
   Of Programmer Z."

Who, you will wonder, is Programmer Z?
You ask your partner, as you dip,
   And he or she,

On the count of three, answers in this wise:
"Ain't he the drip who built this ship?
Some Edgar Rice? Or Vincent Price?
  You know the type I mean."

The program shifts to another scene.
  You have looked at the menu
  And changed your venue,
And now you're a camera high on the boom
  Above the *Belle's* main hatch.

You pan to a porthole and into a room
  As someone lights a match,
And by its flare you see the hair
  Of the figure whom
  It is your doom
To love to the end of the game.
But *only* the hair, and some underwear,
  And part of a picture frame,
And under the frame in a gold cartouche
The name of your nemesis, Programmer Z.

As the flame expires you think you can see
Two cigarettes glowing, or is it three,
And then, so soft you scarcely hear it,
A sound you believe is the sound of a douche,
But when you try to zoom in near it,
The moon turns dark, and the cursor fades,
And the purser brings you a scented letter:
"You've lost again but you're getting better.
Sincerely, 20th Century Fox Arcades."

Orientating Mr. Blank

for Marjorie Perloff

This will be your office, Mr. Blank,
While you remain attached to the Poetry
Division of the Department of Mediocrity.
Prose is down the hall, but we *all* work together—
Except for the two snobs upstairs in Innovation,
Who pretty much stick to themselves.

Now as to categories: Gays are by themselves,
In this drawer. Women who fill in their name blank
With "Ms." go in the Minority file (Drubb's innovation).
Don't file all the drug abusers under Nature Poetry.
Some are Deep Image; others get lumped, together
With younger academics, into regions. Mediocrity

Is *not* randomly distributed. True mediocrity,
Like genius, aggregates into nodes. By themselves
A dozen mediocrities amount to nothing, but put them together
And you have a department. You laugh, Mr. Blank,
But I am always serious when I speak of poetry.
What's New Under the Sun? as Mailer wrote, and innovation

Isn't the answer! The only *genuine* innovation
In the arts has been the belated recognition accorded mediocrity.
By forming poets into Schools and Offices of Poetry,
By helping them most generously to help themselves,
By encouraging their applications to all forms of application
    blank,
They're made to learn that only by colluding together

Can poets obtain the object of money. Together-
Ness! "One Tribe, One Wall"—that was the first innovation
Of burghers in their boroughs, and now, Mr. Blank,
It is the last. Artists now see in their *united* mediocrity
A means toward the Golden Mean, and in themselves
A collective force for forming—and *re*-forming poetry

Into a once-more-*useful* social institution. Poetry
Is no longer the mere serial stringing-together
Of *aperçus* into prosodic masses, those masses themselves
To be collected in a book—even such a book as *The Innovation
Sheaves* (on which, by the by, I wrote my dissertation,
    "Mediocrity
In the work of Ezra Pound")! Well, Mr. Blank,

I hope that you and Mrs. Blank can come to our Poetry
Day Raffle. If not, Mediocrity often has a little get-together.
Usually *without* that pair from Innovation. They stick to
    themselves.

In the News

Last night I dreamt that Bernhard Goetz
    Was slumming in Bhopal,
And the Vatican Bank was taking bets
    On who'll succeed Pope Paul.

Arkansas teachers were cheating on tests
    To see if they had AIDS,
And the Bronx was issuing bulletproof vests
    To students in lower grades.

The weather was warm, and interest rates
    Were climbing higher and higher,
Because some U.S. consulates
    Were said to be on fire.

A bomb had fallen on southern France,
    And for a second time
The nation had renewed the grants
    Of families in major crime.

La Venganza de los Muertos Vivientes

Return to your villages. We won't kill you anymore.
—a Guatemalan general quoted on the evening news

The dead considered whether this promise
could be trusted. They did miss the life
of the village, the cheerful music blasting
from the loudspeaker in the square,
the bustle of the soldiers, the sense
of being part of a drama the whole world
was watching. But they'd grown confused
there in the mass grave, uncertain,
shy. And if they did return,
what could they do, being dead?
Spy on surviving relatives? Live like lizards
in the crevices of walls? *Quien sabe*,
maybe they should just stay planted
where they were, learning ecology.

But the general had summoned them—
they had no choice. They pushed their way up
through the teeming topsoil to emerge
into the Technicolor day, looking exactly
as you'd imagine. And not, of course, able
to repress the natural instinct
of corpses in this classic situation.
Even the withered *abuelita*—"Granny" to us
gringoes—must gnaw at the young corporal's
shinbone; such is the law of retribution.
So what can we do, up here in the north,
to mend matters? I've no idea—
but the President has suggested we send
arms and advisors to help stop the killing.

Lives of Great Men All Remind Us

As the weather wears them down,
These our most brazen men about town
Remind us of the common fate
That's theirs who only meditate,
Erect in parks or slouched inert
On pedestals where squirrels flirt
And pigeons drop their daily poop.
Ah, what a sad, discolored troupe!

Down from his beard, across his chest,
The rains have darkened Lincoln's vest,
As though he had been vomiting
All through winter and into spring,
And Washington upon his horse
Suffers as visible remorse—
Witness those seeming tracks of tears
Across his cheeks and down his ears.

All bronze thus mourns the nation's fate
And heeds, in silence, its debate.

Ancient Hero

Before I watch his wedding
   To the bride his deeds have won,
May I ask to see the bedding
   Over which the blood has run?
May I witness the beheading
   Of his daughter and his son?

Before I run away and hide
   From the arrows of his eyes,
Tell me—does he still reside
   In ballads and in lullabies?
Is it safe to mock his pride
   Within the walls of my disguise?

Love and Clover: A White Paper

Surely the burrow is in an incredible flurry
With the rain yesterday and the cold today
O my brothers I want us to be exactly as we were
In the year of our first calendar
In the safety of those pure silences snuggling
No scents for acres but the reassuring spoor
Of family friends and neighbors

Let us lick each other's noses now remembering
The curve of the root through the living room wall
The games at recess of Hide and Escape
When the schoolyard seemed one seamless lawn
To pasture and lollop about upon
Alas that was long ago alas as we did not know
That the rain would come with such terrible force
To be followed by such penetrating cold

Dear lads we must not be defeated
We must organize a committee we must analyze
Trends in the distribution of grass and predators
We must achieve new levels of trust and security
And though the nights are dark with the gossip of owls
And though the sun only serves to detect
The increasing prevalence of this or that threat
Yet this above all we must not forget
"Love one another or die"
Words to be chiseled on every root
And written across the sky

Events of the Day

A coup was attempted a month ago
In far-away Khartoum,
And now, according to Omdurman Radio,
Eighty-one rebels have met their doom,
And loyalist forces are back in control.

Elsewhere, the Thompson River has taken a toll
Of over a hundred lives, as flood
Waters covered the valley with mountains of mud.
Now the waters are back in their banks,
For which Colorado gives thanks.

Meanwhile on Mars our Viking probe
Has broken its arm for the second time,
And as of this hour it isn't known
If the soil of our sister globe
Is acid or lime,
And whether, by inference, we are alone,
As most scientists seem to fear,
Riding the void on a rotating sphere.

Here on Bermuda the news is less dire:
A goat named Eve was caught in the mire,
And though the *Gazette* says it's still touch and go
Whether they'll get the tar off her or no,
I and the rest of Bermuda believe
In the survival of our dear Eve.

There Is an Index by First Lines

Tom Disch is the author of *The M.D.: A Horror Story* and many other works of fiction. His verse play *The Cardinal Detoxes* has been the focus of recent controversy. This is his seventh book of poetry.

Designed by Martha Farlow
Composed by Blue Heron Typesetters, in ITC Gamma
Printed by The Maple Press Company, Inc., on 55-lb. Sebago Cream